"I LIKE... every 1... said.

Liss was stunned by the sudden volley of revelations. "Umm—how do you feel about sassy women employers?"

"Why don't I just show you?" He said it so innocently, she didn't realize what he intended to do until she was lying beneath him in the soft grass. She stared up at him, surprised, wary. Excited.

"What are you doing?" she gasped, her throat suddenly dry as parchment.

"I'm not *doing* anything. But I'm *planning* on kissing you."

He didn't move, though—merely kept his mouth so close to hers that Liss had to lower her lashes to keep from staring him in the eye. She was intensely aware of his longer, stronger body on top of hers, the firm feel of his muscled thighs on hers, the heat of his flesh against hers.

"This isn't your way of getting even, is it?" Liss asked.

"Actually," he said, his lips brushing hers, inciting every cell in her body to riot, "it's just my way of telling you I want to get to know you better. . . ."

WHAT ARE *LOVESWEPT* ROMANCES?

They are stories of true romance and touching emotion. We believe those two very important ingredients are constants in our highly sensual and very believable stories in the LOVESWEPT line. Our goal is to give you, the reader, stories of consistently high quality that may sometimes make you laugh, sometimes make you cry, but are always fresh and creative and contain many delightful surprises within their pages.

Most romance fans read an enormous number of books. Those they truly love, they keep. Others may be traded with friends and soon forgotten. We hope that each LOVE-SWEPT romance will be a treasure—a "keeper." We will always try to publish

LOVE STORIES YOU'LL NEVER FORGET
BY AUTHORS YOU'LL ALWAYS REMEMBER

The Editors

Loveswept 739

TASTING TROUBLE

ELAINE LAKSO

BANTAM BOOKS
NEW YORK · TORONTO · LONDON · SYDNEY · AUCKLAND

TASTING TROUBLE
A Bantam Book / May 1995

*If you would be interested in receiving protective vinyl covers for your
Loveswept books, please write to this address for information:*

> Loveswept
> Bantam Books
> P.O. Box 985
> Hicksville, NY 11802

ISBN 0-553-44423-9

Published simultaneously in the United States and Canada

*Bantam Books are published by Bantam Books, a division of Bantam Dou-
bleday Dell Publishing Group, Inc. Its trademark, consisting of the words
"Bantam Books" and the portrayal of a rooster, is Registered in U.S. Patent
and Trademark Office and in other countries. Marca Registrada. Bantam
Books, 1540 Broadway, New York, New York 10036.*

PRINTED IN THE UNITED STATES OF AMERICA

OPM   10 9 8 7 6 5 4 3 2 1

To my sister Arlene,
and to Alan. Always.

ONE

If anything else went wrong that evening, Liss Harding thought, she was going to kick something. Preferably the impossibly temperamental stove that couldn't decide if it was going to work or not. Again. The only reason she hadn't kicked it already was because her feet hurt too much.

Forced into the role of cook because her chef, Anthony, had the flu, Liss sighed in exasperation as she rapidly stirred milk into a batch of cheese sauce. The sauce had started to congeal because the unit under the pan was barely putting out enough heat to melt ice. Hearing a noise behind her, she glanced over her shoulder. Her brother-in-law, Rob, who was filling in for the maître d', who was also out with the flu, sauntered into the aroma-filled kitchen with a bemused look on his face.

Liss steeled herself. "I'm afraid to ask, but I will anyway. What's wrong now?"

Rob gave her a suspiciously cheerful grin. "Nothing earth-shattering. At least, nothing a trained waitress or two couldn't cure."

Liss thought of the eager, if somewhat flighty, girl she'd just hired. "Mary Lee?"

"Mary Lee," Rob confirmed.

Liss sighed in resignation. "What did she do now?"

Rob watched her mix butter into a vat of whipped potatoes. "She nearly dumped a bowl of salad in the mayor's lap."

"That sounds like cause for celebration, not concern."

Rob picked up a whisk and stirred the cheese sauce. "I thought so too. Until she tried to refill the water glasses and drenched the tablecloth instead."

"Lord." Liss repositioned the two-sizes-too-big chef's hat that was falling over her forehead. "What did you do?"

"What you told me to when things go wrong. I apologized profusely and told the mayor his and his wife's meals were on the house. Does Mary Lee do this sort of thing often?"

"Often enough," Liss said, thinking of how many free meals she'd given away in the past week.

Peering at the lukewarm unit under the pan, Rob frowned at the stove. "What's wrong with this thing? I thought you just got it fixed."

Liss pulled two foil-wrapped baked potatoes out of the oven. "I did. It just doesn't like to stay fixed. Shouldn't you be in the dining room?"

"Things are slow. Annie's covering for me. You know, you'd make a much bigger profit if you didn't have to keep giving away free meals because your customers have to dodge ice water. Why don't you save yourself a lot of grief and hire an experienced wait-ress?"

"Because I can't pay them what they deserve. And because Mary Lee's trying to save money for college. She'll get the hang of things eventually."

Rob shook his head. "You're too softhearted for your own good."

Shrugging, Liss arranged apple-slice garnishes on two more plates. She'd normally use parsley, but her produce supplier had failed to show up that afternoon. "Someone has to give her a job."

Rob snatched a piece of apple and bit into it. "Ray wouldn't have."

Thinking of her late husband, Liss countered, "Yes, he would have." It might have taken some per-suasion on her part, but he would have.

They both stopped talking as Mary Lee dashed into the kitchen, grabbed a handful of paper towels, and dashed out again.

Rob rolled his eyes. "There goes another dinner tab. You know, Mary Lee's so sweet and innocent looking, you ought to consider using her as your se-cret weapon."

Liss scanned the orders in front of her. "Against who?"

"Farr. Who else?"

Farr. Just the mention of the man's name was enough to send Liss's blood pressure through the roof. The new restaurant critic for the local newspa-per, J. P. Farr had, in six short months, become the bane of all the restaurateurs in the area, mostly be-cause he specialized in scathing reviews, and even mi-nor offenses could inspire one.

Liss turned a steak on the grill. "The way things

have been going tonight, I fully expect him to show up any second now."

"The man does seem to have some sort of sixth sense about showing up when he's least wanted," Rob said.

Liss snorted. "I didn't think he was ever wanted, anywhere, anytime."

"True." Rob paused. "Too bad we don't know what he looks like. I read somewhere that he maintains his anonymity so he can critique restaurants without having them cater to him when he appears."

Liss slathered teriyaki sauce on the steak. "Are you kidding? More likely he insists on anonymity so he doesn't get shot by an irate restaurant owner who's gotten a bad review. Better yet—poisoned by one."

"I take it you saw last week's review of the Firestone."

Liss wrinkled her nose. "I didn't have to. Martha Grey called me right after it appeared. She cried into the phone for a full hour."

"A one-fork rating isn't going to do them any good. Do you think they'll go out of business?"

"If they fold, we'll all know who's to blame." Liss turned to chop onions with a large, exquisitely sharp knife, and imagined J. P. Farr's neck under the blade. "I'd like to meet the man face-to-face and tell him exactly what I think of him," she added, hacking a piece of onion with relish.

"Just as long as he stays away from here tonight," Rob said, heading back to the dining room. "Or we'll all be on the street looking for new jobs."

❖━━━━❖

On a scale of five, Joshua Farrington decided, the Lakeview Restaurant rated a two, and even that was being generous. He shook his head as he surveyed the spacious interior of the Lakeview, illuminated—wrongly, in his opinion—with harsh, unflattering lights that made even the healthiest-looking patrons appear faintly green.

It wasn't that the Lakeview was bad. It was just so blessed ordinary. Pocketing his pen and notebook, Josh picked up his fork and sifted through his lettuce, cucumber, and tomato salad with a distinct lack of enthusiasm.

When he'd come to review the Lakeview he'd honestly had high hopes. So far, though, he wasn't impressed by the food, the service, or the ambience, this last of which was virtually nonexistent. He'd seen subway stations in New York with more character.

That part, at least, had surprised him. The building itself was a gem—a turn-of-the-century Victorian in reasonably good shape, sitting right on the shore of Seneca Lake. A building of stately grace, and one of the few with such distinctive architectural features in this part of upstate New York, it had fantastic potential—which the owner had ignored.

All of the small touches that made a restaurant special, in his opinion, had been ignored as well. Though he suspected the Lakeview was striving for elegance, the napkins were paper, albeit decent-quality ones. The tablecloths were cloth, but, horror of horrors, were covered by a thick sheet of Plexiglas. There wasn't a fresh flower, or any greenery for that matter, in sight. And the menu! It looked as if it had been designed by a first-year art student, and the selection of entrées was, to be kind, boring.

Surreptitiously sliding his small notebook from his jacket pocket, Josh jotted down another comment, careful to check that no one was watching. It was imperative to him that no one realize what he was doing, or who he was. Because he wanted to judge local eateries by what they served everyone, not just him, he guarded his anonymity the way most people guarded their money. His reputation was at stake.

Dessert arrived. Nearly giving up hope for anything that would justify upping his evaluation to a respectable three forks, Josh sampled the chocolate amaretto cheesecake and was more than just pleasantly surprised. The texture was luxuriously rich and creamy, and the sharpness of the dark chocolate was complemented, not overpowered, by the subtle flavor of almond.

Josh stared at the confection, drizzled with amaretto and decorated with a small blossom made of slivered almonds and white chocolate. Unlike the rest of his meal, the dessert was delectable and showed distinct flair.

Rethinking his review, Josh considered his overall impression. With minor touches the beef bourguignon might have transcended the category of merely beef stew. But, unfortunately, both the salad and the soup seemed to have been made by the culinary-impaired. The evening's only saving grace had been the cheesecake.

Wondering how the Lakeview had managed to procure a decent pastry chef, and who he or she was, Josh pushed away his plate.

"Is something wrong with your dessert, sir?"

Mentally making a note not to be so obviously disgruntled about a meal in the future, Josh turned toward the speaker. It was his waitress, a cheerful, if not particularly well-coordinated young lady. So far she'd managed to spill water, drop silverware, and mix up at least two orders that he was aware of—and it was barely eight o'clock.

Josh studied the anxiously smiling girl. He hated to disillusion someone so obviously young and inexperienced, but there it was. It was time for the "Farr Test."

Not content with simply judging the food of an establishment, Josh liked challenging restaurants to do their best in difficult circumstances. An excellent restaurant, faced with a problem, invariably came up with a workable solution, while a run-of-the-mill one almost always managed to make a bad situation worse.

Josh enjoyed creating a bit of trouble to see how a restaurant handled it. Actually, he relished it. Some of his most interesting reviews had come from instances when he'd purposely put a fly in the ointment. Or, more relevantly, in the soup.

This time he was interested in seeing how the staff, which he suspected was well-meaning but woefully undertrained, would handle a nonpaying customer. He gave the waitress his most dazzling smile and tried not to feel guilty for what he was about to do to her faith in mankind.

"The cheesecake is fine," he said truthfully, "but I'd like something to go with it."

The girl frowned, clearly puzzled. "Do you mean, you'd like something to go on top of it? Like whipped cream?"

Tempted to ask for sprinkles just to see how she would deal with the request, Josh smiled again. "Actually, I was thinking more of cappuccino. And the check, too, if you don't mind."

"We don't have cappuccino," she said. Josh was not surprised. "Will coffee do?"

"Coffee will be fine."

It arrived, steaming hot and deliciously rich. Considering adding a half fork to his rating of two, Josh took his time drinking it as he watched the maître d', who looked like no headwaiter he'd ever seen. In fact, he looked like no waiter, period. He looked harried and uncomfortable, like someone's brother who'd been asked to chaperon a pajama party of teenage girls.

Waiting until he was fairly sure the room was as full of patrons as it was going to get on a Thursday night, Josh signaled for his waitress.

Smiling as she approached, she looked from the check, still sitting on the small plastic oblong tray all by its lonesome, to him. "Is something wrong?"

"Actually, yes." Josh did his best to look embarrassed. "I can't pay."

The girl hesitated. "You mean, you've forgotten your wallet?"

"No, I mean I don't have any money."

"That's okay," the girl said. "We take credit cards."

Josh used his most charming smile. "I'm afraid you don't understand. I don't have any cash. And I don't have any credit cards. I am, in a word, broke."

The waitress looked at him in obvious dismay. "Really?"

"Really. I'm sorry. But there it is."

"Oh. Well." Clearly not knowing what to do, the waitress bit her lip. "I guess I'd better go talk to Liss."

Two steps away she glanced back at him in sudden suspicion. "You won't leave, will you?"

"Wouldn't dream of it," Josh assured her.

Three minutes ticked by. Half anticipating a fracas, Josh tensed as the young maître d', having emerged from the kitchen, approached his table. "Sir?" he said politely. "The owner would like to talk to you. Would you mind coming back to the kitchen?"

The owner clearly couldn't be bothered to come to the dining room to address a problem. Not favorably impressed, Josh hid his displeasure as he rose slowly to his feet and followed the younger man through the swinging door at the rear of the dining room.

He had a fleeting feeling of misgiving as he left the safety of the public room. The last time he'd tried this particular ploy, he'd all but gotten kicked out into a back alley by a surly waiter with biceps the size of tree trunks. The incident had netted him a sprained wrist, and that particular restaurant a less-than-favorable review for "service." And even though this particular maître d' wasn't as tall or as muscular as Josh himself was, Josh recognized a distinct air of protectiveness in the young man's demeanor. That might, or might not, mean trouble.

Having visions of being booted out the kitchen door, Josh wasn't quite sure what to expect as he walked into the kitchen. But the slim blond woman wearing a ridiculously oversized white chef's hat wasn't it. She was maybe five-foot-two, and if she weighed more than a hundred pounds he'd eat the apple slices she'd apparently put on his plate.

"Liss?" Hovering close enough to Josh to make

him wary, the young man raised his voice above the sizzle of frying potatoes. "This is him."

Looking too young to be the owner, and too small to boot anyone anywhere, the attractive blonde turned away from a steaming pot toward Josh. The instant her gray-blue eyes met his, Josh knew that whatever else she was, Liss Harding was no one's fool. And he immediately felt a surge of pleasant anticipation.

Laying down the spoon she was holding, Liss hoped she didn't look as dumbfounded as she felt as she faced the virile, attractive man Rob had escorted from the dining room. *This* was the "older guy, down on his luck" Mary Lee had said couldn't pay for his dinner?

Forgetting that Mary Lee was barely nineteen herself, Liss had expected to be confronted with a frail, underfed, somewhat seedy-looking male in his eighties. Instead, the man standing in her kitchen was tall, tanned, somewhere in his midthirties, and about as frail looking as a Mack truck.

"I understand there's a problem," she said neutrally.

"I'm afraid so," he answered in an enticingly deep, well-modulated voice that made Liss wonder if he was some sort of TV personality. "As I explained to the young lady serving me . . ."

Taking in his neatly clipped brown hair, chiseled features, and intense brown eyes, Liss listened as he reiterated his claim that he couldn't pay for his dinner because he had no funds. Though she wasn't an overly suspicious woman, his recitation struck her as oddly smooth and well rehearsed. Was this some sort of local "Candid Camera" routine for one of the area's television stations?

She turned to yank a basket of french fries out of a vat of hot oil, then looked back at the man. Taking her time, she gave his starchy white shirt, burgundy silk tie, and three-piece gray suit a thorough perusal, trying not to notice the trim muscular body beneath the clothes.

"Are you saying you don't have any money *on* you?" she asked. She would have guessed that his suit and his shiny black loafers probably cost more than she spent on clothes in an entire year. "Or that you don't have any money period?"

His quick flashing smile did nothing to dissolve her growing suspicion. "I'm currently broke," he confided. "I know how it must look. But the clothes are from my days in New York, before I moved upstate. I've had them for years. Quality lasts," he added, in a way that made Liss think he'd decided she wouldn't know quality if it came up and stepped on her toes.

Which meant he'd probably taken a good look at her nondesigner black slacks and the white shirt beneath her apron, as well as the furnishings in the dining room. Despite her efforts with Plexiglas and spot mending, all of them were badly in need of replacement.

"I see," she said. Ignoring the way his dark gaze had settled on her mouth, Liss flipped over two steaks. "And did you realize you had no money before, or after, you ordered the most expensive items on the menu?" She tried not to sound accusatory, but didn't succeed very well.

This wouldn't be the first time that someone with

more cash in the bank than she'd ever see in her life-time turned out to be too cheap to pay for his dinner.

The man gave her a knowing smile that made her feel even younger, and more innocent, than she knew she looked. "Before," he admitted. "As long as I was destined for trouble, I figured I might as well be hung for a sheep as a lamb."

Liss raised an eyebrow. "An interesting viewpoint, Mister . . . ?"

"Farrington," he supplied so smoothly, she wondered if it was even his real name. "Joshua Farrington. And you are . . . ?"

She wiped her hands on her apron and extended her right hand. "Liss Harding."

He took his time shaking her hand, studying everything from the pale blond hair tucked under the hat, to her small, upturned nose, to her mouth. His gaze then left her to scan the large kettles she was tending on the stove. "You're the cook?" he asked, glancing at the hat sliding down her forehead.

Liss pushed the oversized chef's hat back into place. "Only temporarily. The chef's out sick. Actually, I'm the owner."

And this man was trouble. Noting that his hands were smooth and cool and well manicured, not callused or dirty, Liss extracted her own damp hand when he didn't let go.

"You're the owner?" he repeated, looking bemused.

"That's right." Knowing she looked closer to sixteen than twenty-six, Liss cocked an eyebrow in challenge. "Does that surprise you?"

His mouth twisted into a half smile. "A little. I thought you'd be a man."

Used to dealing with people who assumed you had to be male in order to run any sort of business other than a hair salon, Liss gave him a saccharine smile. "Life's full of surprises."

"Tonight it is. You're the one who put the spiced apple slices on my plate as garnish, I take it?"

It was a polite query, but considering he hadn't paid for the apple slices in question, and apparently had never had any intention of doing so, it struck Liss as impertinence in the extreme. "Yes," she said, folding her arms across her chest. "I am."

"I guess you've never seen parsley."

"I've seen it," she said evenly as her temperature inched up a few degrees. "Just not recently. My produce man didn't show up as scheduled today. Are you always this cheeky?"

He looked at her in total innocence. "You think I'm being cheeky?"

"Considering I'm the owner and you're a nonpaying customer, yes. Criticizing the cook in her presence is bad enough, but since you haven't paid for your dinner, I'd say it was more than a little cheeky."

"I suppose you think what I did was reprehensible," he said, not looking even slightly abashed by his errant behavior.

"I don't know if it was reprehensible," she said, "but it was certainly dishonest. If you'd come in and told me you were hungry," she added, not bothering to hide her disapproval, "you would have been given a meal. Probably not the expensive one you chose, but it would have certainly kept you from going hungry. Tell me, Mr. Farrington. Do you have a job?"

"My mother keeps telling me I should find gainful employment," he said, smiling wryly.

Just the idea of this particular man being moved to action by a maternal scolding, Liss decided, was laughable.

He looked like the sort of man who figured laws were made to be bent, if not broken. The kind who liked pushing things to the limit. The kind who'd take advantage of a situation so fast, you wouldn't know what hit you.

"I'm sorry if this is awkward," he said.

"You don't *look* sorry."

"I don't?"

"No. You don't." Actually, he looked pleased with himself. And with the situation. Though why he should be was beyond her.

When she didn't speak again, he ventured to say, "I suppose you're going to call the police and have me jailed for theft of services?"

Liss gave him a long look as she contemplated the best way to make Joshua Farrington pay for his expensive dinner and give him a lesson in why "honesty was the best policy." A lesson that she suspected was long overdue. Because if this was the first time he'd pulled this particular stunt, she'd eat her hat.

"No, Mr. Farrington," she said in dulcet tones. "I'm not going to call the police. I don't get mad. I get even."

She could almost see the possibilities flit through his mind as he cocked his head. "Meaning?"

"Meaning, Mr. Farrington . . ." She smiled as an idea blossomed in her mind. "I'm going to give you a job."

TWO

He was looking at her as if she'd just suggested they get married. Which meant, Liss thought with growing amusement, that he'd never dreamed she might offer him a job to work off his debt.

"Doing what?" he finally asked. "Washing dishes?"

"You've been watching too many old movies on television, Mr. Farrington," she said, after shooing a worried-looking Rob back out to the dining room. "We have automatic dishwashers for that sort of thing. Actually, I was thinking of having you do something that takes a little more brainpower."

One of his thick brown eyebrows arched warily. "Like what?"

"Like doing an inventory of the wine cellar."

"Why would you do that?"

She smiled at his open suspicion as she arranged salad on a pair of plates. "Because it needs to be done, of course."

He didn't smile back. "I mean, why would you give me a job?"

"I'm giving you a job," she explained patiently, "because you apparently don't have one. And because you owe me sixty-five dollars and sixty-one cents. Not including Mary Lee's tip."

"I see." He moved closer to her and asked in a smoky, seductive voice, "And just what makes you think you can trust me? For all you know, I could be an escaped felon."

"If you were an escaped felon," she reasoned, looking as employerlike as she could, considering the fact that her hat was slipping again, "the last thing you'd do is tell me so. Anyway, there's only one door in, and out, of the cellar."

His brown gaze leisurely traveled over her. "Meaning?"

Ignoring the strange prickling sensation shooting down to her toes, Liss straightened to her full height and said firmly, "Meaning, Mr. Farrington, if you come out with your pockets bulging, or yourself reeking of alcohol, you can hit the road again."

"Call me Josh." He looked impossibly solemn. "All my instant employers do."

Determined to keep things businesslike, she nodded. "Josh, then. You can call me—"

"After working hours?"

She gave him a smile sweet enough to cause cavities. "Why don't you just call me Liss, like everyone else?"

She'd almost managed to convince herself she'd shown him who was boss, when he gave her a slow smile that had her nape tingling. "Anything you say. Liss."

His drawled reply had a distinctly seductive ring to it. She gave him a quelling look, then blinked in surprise as he removed his suit jacket and laid it over a stool. "What are you doing?"

"Getting ready to pay off my debt," he said. "You *do* want me to repay you, don't you?"

She nodded. "But what has your repaying me got to do with you undressing?"

"This is my only good suit. I don't want to ruin it."

Trying to regain at least some control over the situation, which was deteriorating faster than the speed of light, Liss folded her arms across her chest. "Are you insinuating that you think my wine cellar is dirty?"

He undid the buttons on his vest. "Are you saying it's not?"

"I don't know if it is or not," she admitted, giving up all hope of having a normal conversation with him. "I don't go down there any more than necessary. Are you always this exasperating?"

"No." His smile was innocent and maddening at the same time. "Some of the time I'm merely irritating."

Liss could believe that. "People who steal things irritate me," she informed him.

"I stuck around to confess," he pointed out.

She watched as he removed the vest. "Something tells me you often have good reason to confess."

Neither confirming nor denying her remark, which pretty well confirmed it, he leaned back against the counter and smiled at her. "Does this mean you never want me to darken your door again?"

"No," she said. She was pretty sure that was the reaction he'd meant to elicit with his little striptease. "It means I'd like you to behave in the future. You can get dressed," she added. "It's too late for you to begin tonight."

He shrugged. "If you insist."

She eyed him sternly as he took his time slipping on his vest and jacket. "I do insist. I also insist you pay me back what you owe me." Praying he was honest and trustworthy, even if he couldn't seem to behave himself, she lifted a steak off the grill. "So, what time can you start tomorrow, Josh?"

Parking his car beside the Lakeview the next evening, Josh pocketed his keys and checked his watch. It was seven-fifteen. He was supposed to be writing up his latest review and planning his next one. Instead, he was back at the Lakeview to work off his debt.

He was damned if he knew why.

Deep down he figured it probably had a lot more to do with curiosity about Liss Harding than any real desire to do a more thorough review of her restaurant. It certainly had nothing to do with curiosity about her wine cellar. Not that he hadn't gone to sneaky lengths to see other ones.

On more than one occasion he'd pretended he was looking for the men's room in order to get a peek at a restaurant's wine cellar, but then, those were establishments that merited an in-depth review. He'd already seen more than enough of the Lakeview.

On the other hand, he was fairly sure there was more to Liss Harding than met the eye. Seemingly sweet and innocent, but sassy and savvy at the least expected moments, she'd whetted his interest in a way no woman had for a very long time.

Tonight was a golden opportunity to satisfy his

curiosity about the munchkin, then he'd be on his way. If the wine cellar was no better than the beef bourguignon, he'd be done in less than an hour, then he'd hit the Dockside for dinner and his next review.

Things, however, didn't go exactly as he'd planned.

"Thank heavens you showed up." Clearly relieved to see him, Liss Harding met him at the back door, latched onto his arm, and all but dragged him into the kitchen.

"Did you think I wouldn't come?" he asked, inordinately pleased that she seemed glad to see him.

He'd thought of the blond imp all day, wondering what it would be like to spend an entire evening with her. Her characteristic, if not wholly warranted optimism was a welcome contrast to his own jaded and cynical outlook on life.

"I wasn't sure if you'd show or not," Liss said, leading him through the busy kitchen. "I'm not even sure I should be glad you did, considering how you behaved last night, but there it is. Desperate situations call for desperate measures." She stopped as she noticed the objects in his hand. One blond eyebrow shot up in suspicion.

"What," she asked, sounding exactly like his younger sister when he'd pulled a fast one on her as a kid, "is that?"

"A bouquet of roses," he said, holding it out for her to get a better look at the deep crimson blossoms.

"I know what they're supposed to be. I was asking what *you* think they are. This had better not be an attempt to bribe me," she said in patent disapproval. "Because if you're trying to get on my good side so I'll let you off the hook, you're out of luck."

"This isn't a bribe," he said, trying to look offended, because that's exactly what it had been. A blatant attempt to sweep her off her tiny feet and get her to forgive him for his trespasses. "It's a random act of niceness."

For the first time since he'd met her, Liss Harding looked blank. "It's a what?"

"A random act of niceness," he repeated.

There were a number of variations on the exhortation "Practice random acts of kindness and senseless acts of beauty," but Liss had apparently never been a recipient of any of them.

"Why?" she asked, looking just as suspicious as he'd suspected she would.

"There's no reason. That's why it's random."

"If you say so. What about the candy?" she asked as he handed her both the roses and the box of Godiva chocolates. "Is that random too?"

"No," he said, supremely aware of every perfumed inch of her tiny frame. "That's totally premeditated. It's an apology for me being impertinent last night."

Still looking suspicious, she held the roses to her nose and inhaled their fragrance. "Does this mean you plan to behave yourself tonight, then?"

He smiled. "I wouldn't say that."

"Somehow that's what I thought you'd say." She located a vase and filled it with water. Arranging the flowers, she glanced at him as he came up beside her. "You're something else, you know that?"

"I was thinking the same thing about you." Figuring a little smooth talking was needed to cement the effect of the flowers and candy, he resisted the urge to tuck a fugitive strand of blond hair behind her ear. "Aren't you a little young to be running a restaurant?"

"Aren't you a little old to be out of work?" she countered, stepping away from him.

He swiftly followed until there were barely six inches separating them. "Does my being out of work bother you?"

"Do I look bothered?"

"Actually . . ." She looked ready to bean him with the nearest chair if he moved another inch forward. He studied her, noting that her cheeks were flushed and her French braid was slightly askew. "You look exhausted."

"I am. Talking with you is enough to exhaust anyone. Besides, things have been a little hectic around here."

Hectic sounded like an understatement, Josh decided as he watched Mary Lee, his waitress from the night before, zip into the kitchen, snatch up a roll of paper towels, and zip out again.

"How can you let that girl near hot liquids with a clear conscience?" he asked.

"Don't worry." Liss wrinkled her nose in a way he found unexpectedly charming. "We never let her within reach of soup or coffee. Anyway, this time I think it was just salad hitting the floor."

"Thank God for small wonders."

"Actually," she said, "we can be thankful for large ones as well."

Her tone of voice immediately made him suspicious, but as he started to ask what she meant, he was interrupted by a burst of angry Spanish from a small sturdy man standing by the stove. Wearing a chef's hat, the man muttered *"Madre de Dios"* as he angrily skewered a steak and all but threw it onto the grill. Josh turned to Liss and raised a questioning eyebrow.

"Anthony's not in the best of moods this evening," she said, as though quite used to working with a temperamental chef.

"Ah," Josh said, beginning to wonder what kind of lunatic asylum he'd gotten himself into.

"I need to change your assignment for a while this evening," Liss went on.

"To what?" Josh asked, glancing at the chef again. "Nursemaid?"

Unfazed by the sarcasm, Liss just smiled at him. "No, to temporary maître d'. Rob's car won't start. He's called AAA, but they haven't arrived yet. He said I'd better not expect him anytime soon. And I don't dare leave the kitchen until Anthony's done with his snit fit or the whole place might go up in smoke." She looked hopefully at him.

"Rob is your maître d'?" Josh asked, finding it difficult to keep his eyes off the tiny dimple in her left cheek.

"No. Rob is my husband's brother. Last night he was filling in for my maître d', Peter, who's out with the flu."

Josh couldn't believe how disappointed he was.

He'd assumed—no, hoped—that she wasn't married. Which was stupid, he acknowledged. He shouldn't have any romantic interest in Liss Harding, and for at least two reasons: One, he was in the process of critiquing her restaurant, and not favorably at that; and two, he normally preferred tall, sophisticated brunettes, not sassy, overly optimistic blondes.

Even if he wanted to romance Liss, and he wasn't sure that he did, he'd be the first to admit she wouldn't have let him in the door, let alone into her kitchen, if she knew who he really was.

"I'm not dressed for the public eye," he said. "I thought I was going to be grunging around in the cellar."

In truth, he'd put on jeans and the blue work shirt that he normally saved for weeding his herb garden because he figured they fit his story of being "unemployed and down on his luck" a lot better than the three-piece silk suit had.

"I keep a couple of jackets and ties on hand for Rob when he fills in," Liss said. She seemed unbothered by the fact she had no maître d' on hand, and that the person she wanted to do the job was inappropriately dressed and, as far as she knew, had no notion of how to do it. "You can wear one of those. The jeans will just have to do. Who knows? Maybe we'll start a new fashion in maître d's. Just behave yourself, or Anthony's likely to come after you with a meat cleaver. He gets very protective at times." Then, with a wave toward a small closet near the rear of the kitchen, she went over to retrieve a cake from the cooler.

Left to his own devices, Josh swore under his breath as he stared at the jackets. Now what? The last thing he'd wanted was a job where he'd be facing the public. And in a restaurant yet. You never knew who might walk in the door.

Even though he kept his journalist identity secret, there were still plenty of people who knew him, and who might inadvertently blow his cover.

He should've just paid for the damned dinner and been on his way last night. Or followed through with his usual plan of reimbursing the owner for services rendered the next day.

Trying to think of a sure way to get booted out of

the dining room before he'd begun, Josh picked through the collection of jackets and chose the most offensive one, which was pretty damned offensive, in his opinion.

He held up the brown-and-gray-plaid garment and a gaudy red tie. "Who picked these out for you? Chuckles the clown?"

"No," Liss told him, calmly slicing a raspberry-topped cake into eight equal slices. "My late husband."

Hell and damnation. Josh resisted the urge to crawl under the nearest rug even while the fact that she was widowed, not married, registered in his mind.

"I'm sorry," he said.

"You don't need to apologize." Amazingly quick in the kitchen—at least to Josh, who liked to take his time cooking elaborate gourmet meals for close friends—she shaved dark chocolate onto the cake, checked something in the oven, and arranged mint-leaf garnishes on two parfaits as she spoke. "There's no way you could have known. Anyway, Ray was a great chef, but he would have been the first to admit he was never going to win a spot on anyone's 'best-dressed' list."

Wondering what Ray had been like and how long she'd been married to him, Josh tried to look apologetic. Not too apologetic, though, since he still wanted to get out of working in the dining room. "I didn't mean to be offensive."

"Didn't you?" Liss's smile was wry as she contemplated him. "I thought that was exactly what you were trying to be. It's not going to work," she added as Anthony shot him a menacing look over her shoulder.

Josh tried his best to look blank. "What's not?"

"Trying to get me to throw you out the door before you even get started, of course." She gave him a quick once-over. "Are you wearing the red tie? The blue one would work better with the shirt."

Realizing he still had the crimson tie in his hand, Josh put it back and grabbed the muted blue one. "What makes you think I'm attempting to get myself thrown out?" he asked, trying to figure out how she could look so young and naive, yet seem to know what he was thinking before he did.

"Your determined recalcitrance."

"I'm always recalcitrant."

It was the truth, but not the whole truth. Even though he had a natural tendency to tease people, he usually reserved the heavy-duty treatment for close friends and family. For some reason he felt an especially strong urge to challenge Liss Harding at every turn, just to see what she'd say and do.

He watched her shake her head in resignation. "This should make the evening memorable," she said. "Between you and Mary Lee, we ought to be able to clear out the dining room in no time. Tell me, do you have any idea at all how to be a maître d'?" As she spoke she deftly separated a dozen eggs.

Conceding that he didn't want to see her lose business, which she would if he didn't pitch in, Josh knotted the tie without benefit of a mirror and grabbed a dark blue jacket from the closet. "I think I have the general idea. I greet and seat people. And try to keep everyone happy."

And exactly how he was supposed to do the latter, he thought, with a chef who looked like he wanted to butcher the food instead of cook it, and a waitress who dropped everything she laid her hands on, was beyond him.

Liss kept an eye on Josh Farrington throughout the evening, watching him through the small round window in the swinging kitchen door.

Who on earth was he? she kept wondering. And what was he hiding? Or, more importantly, what didn't he want her to know?

He'd knotted that tie like someone who'd done it all his life, a more telling move than anything else she'd seen so far. But then, instead of being glad of work, he'd done everything but beg her to throw him out the door.

It was ridiculous to think he couldn't get a job somewhere, not to mention a well-paying one. He was charming and self-confident as he greeted the patrons, and he competently seated them so no one waitress ended up with too many customers while another's tables were vacant. In fact, he looked like he'd been born to do the job.

At least, she amended, he had until about an hour earlier. He'd glimpsed her watching him and suddenly become more creative with his seating, putting everyone with light-colored clothes on one side of the room, and those with dark ones on the other. Liss was sure he'd done it because he recognized his credibility was sinking faster than the *Titanic*.

No one could be so totally exasperating without effort, she mused. In fact, it had taken a fair amount of intelligence to be so inept while managing to look totally innocent.

Josh Farrington was many things, Liss decided. But innocent probably wasn't one of them.

So, what the devil was going on?

Was Joshua Farrington really unemployed? And if he was, was there a problem? Something in his background that made him a risky proposition? Something that he'd done, other than being purposely exasperating, that made employers think twice about hiring him?

Of course, Liss conceded, most prospective employers would ask him about his background, unlike her. She grimaced as she thought of how Ray would've shaken his head in dismay at her hiring methods.

They might not be acceptable practice, but they worked for her. She had a sixth sense about people. More important, she had a strong personal desire to help people in need of a job. She might not always pick winners—goodness knows she'd made her share of mistakes in the past year—but she usually recognized the losers. The ones who stole, or simply didn't bother to show up for work.

Josh Farrington was no loser.

Liss felt it with every fiber of her being. He was intelligent. Capable. Personable. Maybe a little too full of mischief and a little too interested in seeing how far he could push her patience. But he was eminently employable by almost anyone's standards. In fact, he was the type of person one fully expected to *be* an employer. The type of person who took charge without thinking.

So what, Liss wondered, was the problem? And, more important, who *was* the man causing such havoc in her dining room?

THREE

She was getting suspicious about him, Josh thought, and he had no one to thank but himself.

Seeing Liss watching him again through the swinging door's porthole window, Josh silently cursed as he seated an elderly couple and wished them a delightful dining experience. How delightful it was going to be was questionable, considering Mary Lee was their waitress, but he'd been doing his damnedest all evening to make sure the Lakeview's customers at least had a safe evening.

Why, he didn't know. If he'd had any brains at all he probably would have let a long line of impatient patrons accumulate, filled all the tables on one side of the room while leaving the other side vacant, and generally acted like someone who didn't have the slightest idea how to keep anyone, let alone an employer, happy.

It would've fit his story a lot better than being capable and efficient, but for some reason he couldn't bring himself to lose Liss Harding any more money than Mary Lee had already managed to.

He'd even shown Mary Lee how to keep from spilling things all over the place. He'd learned, after she'd bumped into him for the umpteenth time, that she had a depth-perception problem on the left side. He'd politely suggested she both serve food and remove soiled dishes on her good side, and to hell with standard restaurant procedure.

It wasn't like him. He didn't normally let himself get involved, on any level, with the owners or any personnel of the restaurants he reviewed. Didn't allow himself to be concerned with their welfare, or whether or not they would lose business after his reviews were published. In one short evening, he'd broken at least half of the rules he'd set up for himself. Why?

After a moment's consideration, he decided to chalk it up to an instant and inexplicable attraction to tiny blond Liss Harding, the antithesis of what he'd formerly thought attracted him in a woman.

Fascinated by her sassy brashness, and especially intrigued by her trusting him enough to hire him when she knew nothing about him—although she was probably regretting that at the moment—he'd already deduced that Liss was generous to a fault.

Take Chester. Please. As a busboy, the kid made a wonderful car mechanic. In fact, Josh was fairly sure he *was* a car mechanic. Or maybe a car thief. He'd been eyeing Josh's prized black Corvette, parked in the front lot where Josh could keep an eye on it, with suspicious interest all night.

And then, of course, there was Mary Lee.

The poor girl seemed to attract trouble. Hell, it seemed to go looking for her. Even though she hadn't spilled anything on him, one young stud in need of an attitude adjustment had gotten particularly nasty toward her. Josh had managed to get the offending clod out the door with a minimum of fuss, an act, he knew, that raised Liss's curiosity another notch higher. Still, he couldn't keep from watching out for Mary Lee, and after they'd closed for the night, he made sure the obnoxious youth was gone before he let Mary Lee head home.

Liss came up to Josh as he watched the taillights of Mary Lee's car disappear into the night. "That was edifying," she said, brushing confectioner's sugar from the sleeve of her black satin blouse.

"Learn anything from it?" Josh asked dryly. He'd already chastised her for overriding his recommendation and allowing the troublemaker into the restaurant in the first place.

"Yes," Liss said as they walked back inside. Though not what she'd wanted to, she admitted. It really wasn't very nice, but being filled with natural curiosity, she'd been trying to trick Josh into some kind of revelation all evening. Much good it had done her.

Vowing not to give up until she'd found out at least something about him, she asked with casual interest, "I don't suppose you were ever involved with law enforcement?"

His quick smile was one of pure amusement. "From what perspective?"

Knowing he wasn't going to answer her, she said, "Helping out Mary Lee was simply more 'random niceness,' I take it."

He lifted his broad shoulders in a shrug. "Mary Lee's a good kid, even if she isn't the most coordinated person in the world. She certainly doesn't deserve to be treated like a doormat by surly studs who could use a few lessons in restaurant etiquette."

"You know what you deserve for what you did tonight?" Liss asked as she checked to see that all the sugar bowls, condiment bottles, and salt-and-pepper shakers had been cleaned and refilled for the next day.

"A kiss and/or your undying gratitude?"

Determined not to let him get the wrong idea just because they were alone in the building, Liss raised a forbidding eyebrow. "I was thinking more of a chance to redeem yourself."

"You think I need to redeem myself?"

"What I think is that I need an objective opinion. And you're the only one here besides me."

"I think I'd rather have a kiss," he murmured in a husky voice that sent prickles of awareness sliding down her spine.

Willing herself not to respond to him, because he was already a handful without any encouragement at all, Liss eyed him with suspicion. "Are you, by any chance, trying to proposition me?"

His brown gaze snagged hers, sending the prickly sensation all the way down to her toes. "Do you want me to proposition you?"

Did she? she wondered. Lord knew, she was attracted to him, though she wasn't sure how that had happened, let alone so swiftly. It was more than a little unsettling. She hadn't so much as looked twice at a man since Ray. Had, frankly, thought she might not ever again feel that crazy pull of awareness, that inexplicable attraction, that had drawn her and Ray together in spite of their differences.

She straightened and tried to put some conviction

into her voice. "I try not to get personally involved with my employees."

It was a lie. She got way too involved with her employees and they both knew it. Josh had seen her loan Mary Lee a hundred dollars just that evening. Liss felt herself flush as he gave her a disbelieving smile.

"I don't suppose we could compromise with an impersonal pat on the back, then?" he said.

"No," she said, "we could not. Actually, I was thinking of letting you sample some of the Lakeview's famous crêpes flambés. *If* you behave yourself for more than twenty seconds in a row."

He removed the borrowed jacket and hung it over a chair. "I didn't know the Lakeview offered any crêpes flambés."

"It doesn't yet. I'm still trying to perfect the recipe."

"Shouldn't that be the chef's job?"

Liss made sure the dead bolt was in place on the front door. "Crêpes aren't exactly Anthony's style."

Josh loosened the knot on his tie. "No, I can see that."

"Anthony's a good chef," she said, watching as Josh removed the tie. "He's just a bit . . . erratic."

"Doesn't that have an 'erratic' effect on his cooking?" Josh asked, undoing the top button of his blue shirt.

It did, but Liss hated to admit it. Instead she watched as Josh rolled the sleeves of his shirt up his muscled forearms. "What are you doing?" she asked.

"Giving back what I borrowed and making myself more comfortable. What's the matter, Liss? Don't you trust me?"

"I'm not sure." She took a deep breath to relieve the tightness in her chest. "You haven't been arrested as a con man or anything recently, have you?"

"I'm as trustworthy as the day is long," he assured her.

And as dangerous as an open flame, she decided. Not to her physical safety, but to her peace of mind. She'd settled into a comfortable existence of work, work, and more work. Joshua Farrington looked like he was ready to unsettle that existence on a second's notice.

"So. Are you going to fire him?"

Somehow, within a matter of seconds, he'd closed the distance between them to about a foot.

Determined to hold him at bay, Liss kept an eye on him while she wrestled with the latch on a window. "Who?"

A good eight or nine inches taller than she was, Josh reached over her head, slid the lock into place, then planted his hand on the wall near her shoulder. "Your 'erratic' chef. Anthony."

He was so close she could feel his body heat straight through her clothes. Wondering if it was her imagination that he mentally undressed her every time he thought her attention was turned elsewhere, Liss ducked under his outstretched arm and moved to the next window. "Whatever for?"

"Considering the way he was flinging food and utensils around tonight, he's an accident waiting to happen."

As she locked the window Liss took a deep bracing breath as Josh followed behind her. "Anthony's a little temperamental, but not dangerous or accident-prone."

"I'm sure your insurance company will be glad to hear that."

"Were you in insurance?" Liss asked, partly to change the subject and partly to find out something, anything, about Josh. She was frustrated that despite numerous efforts, she still knew virtually nothing about him. She could usually get most of a new employee's life history within a matter of two hours. Sometimes within a matter of minutes. But then, she'd never dealt with anyone quite like Josh Farrington.

His voice was wry when he answered her. "No, I'm not, and have never been, in insurance. I've never been an astronaut or brain surgeon, either."

She finished locking all the windows and turned to him. "You're not going to tell me what you did for a living, are you?"

"I wasn't planning on it, no."

"Aren't you a little old to be playing games?" she asked as he followed her across the dining room.

"What game is it that you think I'm playing?"

She turned and looked him squarely in the eye. "This one, for one. Flirting with me for another."

His gaze slid to her mouth. "You think I'm flirting with you?"

She resisted the urge to look at his mouth as he spoke. "In a word, yes. You know, I think I'm beginning to see why you're unemployed. Do you act like this around women employers all the time?"

"I've never had a woman employer before," he said. "Takes some getting used to."

"So do you."

"Do I still get the crêpes flambés?"

"You not only get them . . ." She led the way to

the empty kitchen. "You can watch me make them, if you like."

Josh picked up the jacket and tie as he followed her. "If you're half as entertaining as Anthony in the kitchen, I ought to have brought my video camera."

"No one is as entertaining in the kitchen as Anthony." She eyed him as he hung up the jacket. "If you're without funds, how come you have a video camera?"

He turned and faced her. "I don't. I was joking. What's the matter, Liss?" he chided in a way that created an instant intimacy between them. "Don't you believe me?"

"How can I believe or not believe? You haven't told me anything yet." Determined not to let him sidetrack her, she studied him over the counter as she brought out a bowl. "Can I ask you something?"

"What do you want to know? My checkbook balance?"

"I don't need to know your checkbook balance. I already have plans on how to exact payment from you for your misbehavior." She pulled a whisk from a drawer. "Why are you so bitter?"

He raised an eyebrow as he perched on a stool. "Do I look like I'm bitter?"

"Do you always answer questions with more questions when you don't want to provide answers?"

"Do you think I'm avoiding answering?"

"Considering you haven't answered me yet, yes."

"I guess I'm a little bitter," he said after a moment. She gathered ingredients and set them on the counter. "About anything in particular? Or just everything in general?"

Josh watched her with a mixture of amusement

and wariness. He knew he'd be treading on thin ice if he told her too much about himself, but he figured she'd earned the right to ask, if for no other reason than for not hitting him over the head for his creative seating arrangements that evening.

Still, he couldn't help hesitating before admitting, "If I seem bitter, it's because I once had something that meant a lot to me, and I gave it away, without a fight, because it was the expedient thing to do."

Liss dug out a spoon from a drawer. "Can you get it back again?"

Josh thought of the beloved restaurant he'd started up from nothing in Manhattan. It wasn't just that he'd let Moira have it that ate at him. It was the fact that she hadn't really wanted it, except as a way to get to him. She'd wanted the last laugh. And she'd gotten it, running La Petite Maison into the ground, until it closed less than three months after he'd left New York.

"No," he finally said. "I can't get it back." Not that he didn't have plans for his future. He just couldn't tell Liss Harding what they were. Or who he was.

Remembering his meal from the evening before, and why he'd been eating it in the first place, Josh studied Liss's quick hands and rapt expression as she mixed the dry ingredients for the crêpe batter. "You look like you're in your element," he said, beginning to recognize that the Lakeview's saving grace—its pastry chef—might also be the same person who'd apparently concocted that thoroughly mediocre beef bourguignon he'd eaten. "Been doing this sort of thing long?"

Liss shrugged. "I'm reasonably competent in the kitchen."

But she'd never had any formal training. And she wasn't naturally talented the way Ray had been, except when it came to confections. Consequently, she'd had to simplify the Lakeview's menu after Ray died, because when her chef was out sick she needed to take over herself.

"Ray was the chef in the family," she explained, trying not to look nervous as Josh came up beside her. "He was the one who wanted to open a restaurant in the first place. All our friends told us we should, since Ray not only liked cooking, he was terrific at it."

Josh watched her pour liquid over the shrimp she was sautéing in butter. "Do you like cooking?"

She glanced up at him, smiling wryly. "Actually, I do. I just don't get time to relax and enjoy it much anymore. In any case, I'm a lot more comfortable making desserts than main dishes." Which was why she was trying a new entrée now. If she couldn't get the hang of it, she couldn't offer it except when her chef was on the job. "Why do I get the feeling you want to ask me something personal?"

He gave her an innocent look. "Because you're a suspicious woman?"

"A woman would have to be a fool not to be suspicious around someone as evasive as you. What do you want to know?"

He helped cut up garlic. "I was just wondering where you got the recipe for the beef bourguignon you made last night."

She eyed him thoughtfully. "Why do you want to know?"

"Natural curiosity?"

Sincerely doubting that, Liss watched him slice the clove of garlic with swift, sure strokes. "It's a variation of one of Ray's recipes." She didn't add that Ray's version was so complicated she always felt like she needed an engineering degree to make it.

"Would it offend you if I suggested something?"

She grabbed another bowl and set it on the counter. "I guess that would depend on whether your suggestion has anything to do with my employment practices or my cooking techniques."

"Such a suspicious woman," he scolded. "I was going to suggest that the beef bourguignon would be more interesting if you seasoned it a bit more."

Liss was too surprised to speak at first. Sensing she was about to find out something important about him, whether he intended it or not, she finally asked, "What would you suggest?"

He named a spice she'd never heard of. "I don't think I have that," she said, wondering if it was her imagination that he suddenly looked very much at home in her kitchen. "Would something else work?"

"It would help if I knew what you had." She moved aside so he could search the spice rack for a suitable substitute. After a moment, he handed her a small jar. "Try that," he suggested.

"You used to be involved in running a restaurant, didn't you?" she said.

Even though she was looking at the spice jar and not at him, Liss could feel him smiling at her latest ploy. "I suspect everyone in New York has worked in a restaurant at one time or another," he said. "Especially all the actors. Ever been to New York?"

Aware that he'd smoothly changed the subject— again—Liss speculated on whether he was an actor.

That would explain why his mother thought he ought to find a "real job."

"Only once," she answered. "Nearly scared the pants off me."

"I wish I'd been there."

"So you could have reassured me?"

"Hell, no. So I could've seen you with your pants scared off you." Smiling at her withering look, he leaned against the counter. "You don't strike me as the type of woman who's easily frightened."

Ignoring the way her heart was starting to tap-dance at his closeness, Liss added a stream of milk to the dry ingredients, then whipped the thin crêpe batter until it was smooth. "I'm not. I was only ten when my folks took me there. How long did you live in New York?"

"Long enough to know I didn't want to grow old there. Or raise kids there."

Liss's interest perked. "Do you have any? Kids, I mean?"

His voice held a glimmer of amusement. "You're persistent, aren't you?"

She dropped a bead of water into a hot frying pan to test the temperature. "You mean nosy."

"That too. You wouldn't be trying to pump me for information again, would you?"

She couldn't help smiling. "I might be. So, do you? Have kids?"

"No. Do you?"

"No." She poured a thin layer of batter into the pan. "Ray and I were going to wait to start a family until after we got the restaurant on its feet."

"When did he die? If you don't mind me asking."

Liss felt her throat ache, as it always did when she

thought about how Ray's life had been cut short. "A year ago. In a boating accident. He was determined to catch the biggest fish in the Lake Trout Derby, regardless of how bad the weather got." And it had gotten very, very bad, thanks to a storm that had whipped up without warning.

"Ray had lots of ideas for improving the Lakeview," she added.

"I get the feeling you have a few ideas for improvement yourself."

"Really?" She deftly flipped the cooked crêpe out of the pan and poured another. "I get the same feeling about you."

"Me? Why?"

"You keep looking at things like you'd like to change them."

"I wasn't aware I was being so obvious," he said blandly. "I guess I'm a born renovator."

Liss nodded. "I like changing and remodeling things myself."

"Seeing who you hire as employees, I can believe that."

"All they need is a little guidance. And a little training."

"Is that why you insisted I come back tonight?" he asked, sounding amused. "To try to change me? Give me a little guidance?"

"I'd have to know what I was changing you from, in order to know what I was changing you to, now, wouldn't I? And since you haven't exactly been forthcoming about who you are, what you've done, or where you come from . . ."

Josh didn't mean for it to happen. He wanted to get her mind off that particular tack, but when she turned around suddenly, a sassy smile on her face, he forgot all about why he should keep some distance between himself and Liss. He didn't even stop to think about what he was doing. He simply leaned over and kissed her.

FOUR

It was a sweet exploratory kiss, his mouth pressing gently against hers for the barest moment in time, before he straightened.

Stunned by both the action and her soul-rocking reaction to him, Liss stared at him wide-eyed as she felt her body clamoring for even closer contact. "What was that for?" she finally managed to ask.

His brown eyes locked onto hers, sending a flurry of hot impulses hopscotching through her veins. "I thought you wanted me to. Was I wrong?"

No, she thought, feeling as if she would burst into flame if he touched her. He wasn't wrong, but the kiss was. All wrong. She couldn't afford to complicate things by getting romantically involved with one of her employees.

No, that was a lie. It was him, in particular, she didn't think she should get involved with. Whether it was a girlfriend or, heaven forbid, a wife, or some-thing sinister in his background that he was hiding, he wasn't telling her something important. She knew it as surely as she was standing there.

"I don't think it's wise for us to let our relationship get too personal," she said, halfway wishing the kiss had never happened. And halfway wishing it had been a lot longer, and a lot more thorough.

His voice was low. "And do you always do what's wise, Liss?"

"Not always," she admitted. She knew he was thinking not just of the way she'd started to kiss him back, but of how she'd hired him virtually off the street when she knew nothing about him. "But I like to think I have some common sense. You might try cultivating some yourself," she added, taking a quick step backward as he leaned toward her again.

She expected him to try coaxing her into another embrace, a more intimate one. But, to her surprise, he backed off.

Sliding his hands into his pockets, he studied her with an expression she couldn't even begin to decipher. "I'm sorry if I offended you."

"You didn't offend me," she said truthfully. "You surprised me. I didn't realize you thought of me that way."

"What way?"

She gave him a stern look. "You know what way. As a woman. I thought you thought of me as your employer." In spite of all the flirting and teasing, she honestly hadn't thought he was interested in her. At least, not enough to act on it.

His slow smile made her breath catch. "Right now, how about I think of you as the cook? I'm still waiting for my crêpes flambés." Liss turned back to the stove and took a deep calming breath. "Doesn't your wife mind you kissing other women?" she asked as she splashed warm brandy over the shrimp in the pan.

"I don't have a wife. Or a dog, or a cat, or a bird, or a goldfish. I'm an unattached guy." He edged closer. "How about you?"

Refusing to look at him, in case she hadn't gotten as much control over herself as she thought she had, Liss tipped the pan slightly toward the stove's flame, setting the brandy aflame. "How about me, what?"

He ran his forefinger lightly down her arm, sending shock waves through her system. "Are you seeing anyone?"

She contemplated lying out of sheer self-preservation and let the shrimp flame for a moment before answering. "No."

Aware of his pleased satisfaction, she stirred in cream, then dished the shrimp onto the crêpes. She rolled them, topped them with more of the cream sauce, and added sprigs of parsley as garnish, then she watched in nervous anticipation as he took the plate from her hands and slowly forked up a bite.

"What do you think?" she asked, exasperated at herself for wanting his approval when, for all she knew, he habitually ate dog food for dinner and loved it.

Looking like a man on a mission, Josh chewed thoughtfully for a moment then said, "It tastes like burned tires."

Liss frowned, not quite believing her ears. "What?"

He licked the fork clean. "I said it tastes like—"

"I heard what you said." Thoroughly offended by his remark, she didn't even think of possible repercussions as she whipped off her apron and threw it at him. "Beast."

He dodged the flying apron with a gracefulness that made her wonder if he was accustomed to being used as a target. Then he caught her arm, pulling her up so that she was nose to nose with him.

"I thought you wanted me to be honest," he said while she stared at him in wide-eyed alarm.

She swallowed. "I did."

"But?"

She licked her dry lips and tried not to think about how close his mouth was to hers.

"But after all the effort I put into this," she said, "the least you could do is soften the blow a little. You're not the violent type, are you?" she asked, aware of the strong fingers still curled around her arm.

"Not as long as it's aprons and not knives that are being aimed my way." His gaze settled on her mouth. "What could I do to soften the bad news?"

She lowered her own gaze to his chin. "Tell me something nice, *then* lower the boom, if you must."

Slowly letting her go, Josh considered her suggestion. He'd automatically given her his honest opinion, the same way he always did when he reviewed a restaurant, because it had never occurred to him to do otherwise.

Surprised, both by her affronted reaction and his own unexpected desire not to hurt her feelings, he thought a moment, then finally said, "The crêpes are nicely done. Unfortunately, the shrimp taste like burned tires. How's that?"

"It's about a one-fork review." Deftly putting some space between them before he could latch onto her again, Liss began clearing the counter.

Josh jerked back, startled by her offhand remark. Despite his efforts to keep her off balance, did she know who he was after all, and was she giving him a chance to come clean on his own?

He looked at her as she placed the dirty dishes in the sink, then said in his most neutral voice, "I beg your pardon?"

Rinsing a bowl, Liss looked up. "Sorry. Bad joke. Don't mind me. I'm a little oversensitive when it comes to criticism. Especially when people award 'forks' instead of providing helpful commentary."

"You dislike someone who gives forks away?" Josh asked, hoping he didn't sound too obtuse.

"You must not read the food section of the local paper," she said. "I'm referring to the caustic restaurant reviews by some pompous self-styled critic named J. P. Farr."

"I see." Trying not to take her remarks personally, the way he always hoped his critiques were accepted by the restaurants he reviewed, Josh paused. "You don't agree with her reviews?"

The remark had been calculated to put Liss off guard, and it succeeded.

She looked at him blankly. "Her?"

"I'm sorry." He smiled in feigned puzzlement. "Is it a man we're talking about?"

Grabbing a towel, Liss dried her hands. "You know, I haven't the foggiest idea. I've always assumed it's a man from the aggressively nasty way the column is written. But I suppose it could be a woman."

Aggressively nasty? Was *that* how she perceived his carefully worded, carefully thought-out reviews?

More than just offended by her derogatory assessment, Josh forced himself to keep the irritation out of his voice. "He—or she—probably doesn't mean to be vindictive. I imagine he's just doing his job."

Liss finished drying her hands, obviously not convinced. "If you say so. Speaking of jobs, we need to talk about yours. What time can you come tomorrow?"

"I'm not coming tomorrow," Josh said, surprised by her question.

She smiled at him. "Of course you are."

"Why 'of course'?" he asked politely.

Equally polite, Liss enlightened him. "Because you owe me for that little stunt you pulled out in the dining room."

"What stunt?"

"You mean, which one, don't you? And then, of course, there's the matter of the stolen kiss. . . ."

"Are you saying you're charging me for that?"

"You didn't think it was free, did you?" Liss asked, thoroughly enjoying the expression on his face.

"If you must know, I wasn't thinking at the time. I was feeling. I gather you think I was being recalcitrant tonight in a number of ways?" As he spoke his hand came up to caress her left earlobe.

Liss stepped out of reach as her heart started climbing into her throat. "I don't think you'd know how to behave if you were given a road map. You don't really expect me to believe that it was just coincidence that you seated everyone with light clothes on one side of the room, and dark on the other?"

"You don't believe in coincidence?"

"I don't believe in a lot of things. Including Santa Claus and the tooth fairy. I especially don't believe in coincidence when it involves you. What, exactly, were you trying to do, anyway?"

He shrugged. "It was too quiet. I thought I'd liven things up."

"Is that why you put Councilman Curtis and his new wife at the table next to his ex-wife?"

"You think that was on purpose?"

"I know it was. You get a particularly innocent look on your face when you're about to pull a fast one. Don't even think about kissing me again," she warned, recognizing the look she was just talking about. "Or I'm going to be forced to show you just how uninnocent I am."

"It would almost be worth risking my neck to see it." He contemplated her in a way that made her glad she'd maneuvered the counter between them. "What exactly would I do if I came back tomorrow? Wait tables?"

"God forbid," she said with feeling. "Trying to imagine you working in any capacity in the dining room gives me the willies. I was thinking you could come back and do an inventory of the wine cellar."

"Why?" he asked.

She smiled at his lack of enthusiasm. "Number one: Because you owe me. Number two: Because it still needs to be done. And number three . . ." She gave him an even sunnier smile. "Because with your color-coding skills, you've demonstrated you at least can tell red wine from white wine."

Which was more than most of her help knew, Josh thought. He'd watched Mary Lee serve asti spumante in lieu of champagne to one irate guest, because it had "bubbles."

"I'm busy tomorrow afternoon," he said sourly, in a blatant attempt to discourage her.

Looking far more amused than discouraged, Liss

shrugged. "Then come in the evening again. It doesn't matter when it's done, as long as it gets done. Although, it probably ought to be done sooner rather than later. Some of the bottles have been down there for close to twenty years, so they probably ought to be drunk."

"Twenty years?" Josh repeated, having the sinking feeling she'd gotten his number, despite her look of guilelessness, and had figured out that the promise of a potentially valuable collection of wine would bring him back faster than ants to a picnic.

"There were dozens of bottles left behind in the cellar by the previous owner," she went on, sounding blithely unconcerned. "A Tim Taylor. You've heard of him?"

Tim Taylor, a local artist, had been one of the area's most avid wine collectors before he'd abandoned all his worldly goods and headed for an ashram in India a few years back.

"Yes," Josh said, feeling like a man who'd stepped into quicksand. "I'm familiar with the name."

"So, does the idea of sorting through his collection appeal to you?"

It did. And so did she. There was something so refreshingly honest about her. So appealingly sassy and optimistic.

"I'll think about it," he said, knowing even as he said it, that he was doomed to spend another evening at the Lakeview.

"How's the inventory coming along?" Liss asked the next evening, when Josh finally emerged from the cellar, after two hours, for a cup of coffee.

It had surprised her when he'd shown up just after seven. She honestly hadn't thought he was going to. From the look of him as he'd given her a dour greeting, then descended into the depths of the wine cellar with her wine inventory notebook in hand, she suspected he wasn't sure why he'd come himself.

Dangerously handsome in black jeans and a black polo shirt, he settled his lean frame on a stool. "I'm about halfway done. And if you think this isn't going to cost you more than flaming crêpes," he added with feigned menace, "you're wrong."

"I was planning on giving you dessert when you're through," she said, decorating a mocha torte with chocolate wafers. "*If* you behave yourself."

He snatched one of the wafers from the counter and ate it. "More of the chocolate amaretto cheesecake?"

Not sure from his casual tone if he was looking forward to it or dreading it—since he'd already criticized both her beef bourguignon and her seafood crêpes flambés—Liss studied him for a moment. "If you want."

His voice dropped to a husky purr. "If I told you what I really want, you'd probably bean me with a skillet."

She frowned in disapproval. "If this is your idea of behaving, what you're likely to get is your just deserts."

"I can't help myself. You turn such an interesting shade of pink every time I tease you." He ate another wafer. "How's Mary Lee doing? Bathed any customers in onion soup yet?"

"We're serving vichyssoise this evening," Liss told him. "I'm not stupid. I am, however, desperate."

"A desperate woman," he murmured, getting up and coming closer. "My favorite kind. What are you desperate for?"

She put her hand squarely in the middle of his chest, stopping him. "Besides an orderly wine cellar and good behavior from you? I need a special wine to serve with roast duckling. I have a young couple on their honeymoon seated at a table in the rear and I'd like you to pick something out that they might enjoy."

He cupped his hand over hers, pressing it against his warm chest. "Are you sure you trust me after last night?"

"I never trust you," she said, sliding her hand out from under his before she had a chance to think about how firmly muscled he was. "Anyway, I figure things couldn't get any worse than they were last night. Unless, of course, you select something that would more properly go on a salad."

Josh tsked at her suspicion. "I never pick on newlyweds. They need all the support they can get. I'll see what I can find." His fingers purposely brushed hers as he took the cup of black coffee she was offering him. "Maybe when you have a chance you'd like to come down and see what I've done."

Determined not to respond to his insistent teasing and touching, Liss took a bracing breath. "Things are starting to wind down. I'll be down in a few minutes."

Even as she said it she wondered if she should take someone along as a chaperon. Goodness knew, Rob would readily volunteer. He'd been giving her pointed looks of disapproval ever since he'd found out she'd not only hired Joshua Farrington, she'd turned him loose in her wine cellar. For the last hour he'd pleaded in vain with her to allow him to escort Josh out the back door.

By evening's end, she couldn't delay going downstairs any longer. Having supervised the cleaning of the kitchen and sent the last of her help on the way, including Rob, with the night's deposit, and Peter the maître d', who was back on the job but looking none too peppy, Liss was turning off lights and locking up when she turned around and found Josh standing in the darkened room behind her.

"Lord, I'd forgotten all about the wine cellar," she lied, knowing perfectly well she hadn't gone downstairs because she didn't trust him—or herself. "Were you waiting for me?"

He shrugged. "I had plenty to keep me busy."

Her smile was rueful. "I'll bet you did. It was a disaster area the last time I looked."

His deep voice was as dry as the Sahara as he walked forward out of the shadows. "And just when was that?"

"Longer than I care to admit. Cellars give me the willies. All the spiderwebs . . ." she shuddered.

"The spiders, and their webs, have been eliminated," Josh told her, quashing any chance of her using that as an excuse not to go down there with him. "And so, apparently, have some of your better vintages. You wouldn't have happened to have hired a kleptomanic by any chance? A number of bottles appear to be unaccounted for."

Liss hated to admit it, but it was the reason she'd had to fire Mary Lee's predecessor. And the reason she'd wanted Josh to do a current inventory. She figured at least half a case of her more expensive stock had been smuggled out the back door.

She gave him a wan smile in answer.

He nodded in wry acknowledgment. "I thought so. You'd give anyone a chance, wouldn't you?" He extended his hand toward her. "Come see what I've done."

"Should I take a stiff drink before I descend the stairs?" she asked, starting to panic at the thought of going into the cellar, alone, with him.

"Do you have a weak heart?" His hand caught hers.

Only around you, she thought, knowing she was getting much too involved with him, considering how little she knew about him.

"I'm disgustingly healthy," she said as her small hand was engulfed by his larger one. And so was he, she thought.

In fact, they were probably both oversexed. Because he was looking at her in exactly the same way she was trying, very hard, not to look at him. Like he wanted to touch her. Kiss her. Make love to her . . .

Liss desperately tried to think of a good reason why she couldn't stay in the cellar for more than three minutes and came up empty.

FIVE

As they descended the stairs Liss thrashed around for something innocuous to think about and talk about. She got it on the fifth step.

"I was wondering what that pounding was," she said, noting that he'd fixed the wobbly step on the wooden stairway.

"You might not sweat the little things," Josh said, referring to the sign on her kitchen wall that advised DON'T SWEAT THE SMALL STUFF, with the additional advisory, IT'S ALL SMALL STUFF, "but I can assure you, your insurance man does. You're lucky none of your employees have tripped and broken their necks. Lawsuits can be costly lessons."

Trying to look chastised, Liss nodded. "I suppose, being a lawyer, you think of things like that."

"If I were a lawyer," he said, falling easily into what was becoming a predictable game between them, "I'd probably be considering sending you a bill for misrepresentation. Because if Tim Taylor actually left anything of worth behind, it went with your former employee. What's wrong?"

Liss had hesitated near the base of the stairs.

"You're sure all the spiders are gone?" she asked, wondering suddenly if she'd made a grave mistake, besides risking her virtue.

What did she know about Joshua Farrington, after all? He hadn't yet come up with so much as a Social Security card. It might not even be his real name. Everyone else was gone. The restaurant was all locked up. It was night. The cellar was the perfect place to commit all sorts of mayhem, involving her.

If his intentions were not only less than honorable, but deadly, no one was going even to notice if she'd gone home or not. She'd walked, rather than bringing her car, which was less reliable at the moment than her stove. No one would even find her body until the next evening when a customer ordered wine. . . .

She must've looked like a deer caught in headlights, she realized, because Josh's demeanor subtly changed.

Standing on the step below her, he faced her. "What's the matter, short stuff? Does being alone with me make you nervous?"

"I'm not nervous," she protested, trying to convince herself that no man who had dastardly deeds on his mind would call her "short stuff." "I'm understandably cautious. You haven't been arrested for murder recently, have you?"

"Trust me." His low voice sent her blood rushing through her veins. "There's nothing down here that will harm you."

"Is that a promise?" she asked, trying for lightness and still managing to sound just as panicky as she felt.

"It's a solemn oath." He smiled as he brushed back a wayward tendril of hair from her cheek. "Nothing's going to happen to you that you don't want to happen."

Which covered a lot of territory, Liss decided, considering what she was feeling for him at the moment. It didn't seem to matter that she knew virtually nothing about him. She liked him. And she wanted to know him better. A lot better.

Determined to get out of the cellar before he figured that out, and acted on it, she smiled brightly. "So. Have you figured out what I need?" Realizing how that sounded, especially after his remark, she added belatedly, "I mean, in the way of wine."

Looking impossibly innocent, considering what was probably going through his mind, Josh nodded. "As a matter of fact, yes. Have a seat," he said, urging her to sit on the newly swept step, "and let me show you what I've done. To start with . . ."

Not sure if he was pulling her leg or not, Liss sat with her chin cupped in her palm and listened in mortified silence as he showed her how he'd sorted the wines according to color, much the way he'd divided her patrons the other night, putting the reds on the left, the whites on the right. Then, as she wondered if she should have kept him out of the cellar after all, he added insult to injury by telling her how he'd alphabetized them. By variety.

He looked expectantly at her. "Any questions?"

The only question she had was how in the dickens was she going to keep from strangling him?

Knowing Rob was going to say "I told you so," she stared at Josh in dismay. "That's it?" she asked, hoping he was just teasing, but fearing he wasn't.

She couldn't believe how disappointed she was. But then, what had she expected? Just because he'd ordered one of the best wines on the wine list two nights earlier didn't mean he knew anything about the stuff. In fact, it might signify nothing other than that he'd ordered that wine because it was also the most expensive.

"No," he said, "that's not it. You've still got some excellent dessert wines left, especially sauternes. Apparently your wine thief didn't know what a Château d'Yquem was."

From what he'd been telling her so far, she'd expected he wouldn't know, either.

Suddenly suspicious of both the offhand remark and his too innocent expression, she asked casually, "What about the reds? Anything worth noting?"

"As a matter of fact, yes. Your wine thief didn't know much about Italian reds, either. He apparently took the Montepulciano d'Abruzzo and left behind the Vino Nobile di Montepulciano, clearly not knowing the difference."

Not knowing the difference herself, Liss just stared at him as he went on, extolling the virtues of the Vino Nobile di Montepulciano, which, Liss gathered, was a heavy, slow-maturing wine, while the Montepulciano d'Abruzzo was cheaper, lighter, and in his opinion, not particularly memorable.

"This is fascinating," she said, finally catching the amused gleam in his eyes. "But is there anything in particular I need?"

Even as she asked it she wondered how Josh Farrington had learned so much about wine. And where. And from whom. And whether his teacher had been a man. Or a woman.

"In my opinion?" he said. "I think you could use another kiss."

"I'm serious," she insisted.

"What makes you think I'm not?"

She sighed in exasperation. "I'm *asking* what you think."

He moved closer. "I think you're beautiful, and intelligent, and infinitely desirable."

"I'm also your employer," she reminded him as she scootched up a step.

"Meaning?"

"Meaning, the only thing I'm going to discuss with you at the moment is wine."

Josh sat next to her. "Discussing wasn't what I had in mind."

Liss forced air into her lungs. "What did you have in mind?"

"What do you think?" He took her hand in his.

She thought she was in deep trouble. Not because he wanted to kiss her again, which she was pretty sure he did. But because she wanted him to.

She removed her hand from his with an effort. "I think we should stick to business, don't you?"

He tweaked her earlobe. "Not really."

"That is because you're not the one trying to figure out how come more of your customers don't order wine. Tell me what I have and what I need. In wine. Before I go out of business."

"You wouldn't be trying to make me feel guilty, would you?"

She lifted an eyebrow. "Is it working?"

As she favored him with a stern look he relented. "You could use more Bordeaux. They're usually big sellers and you've got less than half a case. I'd suggest some of the better châteaus like Lynch-Bages. Or maybe Brane Cantenac. Or even Talbot.

"You'll probably want to stay away from Italian reds like Tignanello and Sassicaia. They're too expensive now that they've been discovered. Come to think of it, Rubesco might be a good choice. It's similar but not so expensive. The wine crowd hasn't caught on to it yet."

Liss blinked at this sudden flood of information. "Are you saying I should run out and buy more wine tomorrow?"

"How much do you know about wine?" he asked, in his usual fashion of answering a question with another question.

"I can tell reds from whites," she said.

"Then I'd suggest you consult someone knowledgeable in the field before you commit a lot of money. If you go by what you have, and simply buy the next year's release, you're going to be in for some nasty surprises. Take this Bordeaux, for instance."

He got up and reached for a bottle on the top rack, and Liss tried not to notice the way his knit shirt stretched tautly over the muscles in his back.

As he went on to explain why the Bordeaux was only average, she contemplated the ease with which he discussed different vintages. Where had he gotten all this knowledge?

Suddenly aware that his attention was focused on her and not on the bottle in his hands, Liss stood up.

"Is there anything else before we close up shop?"

He inclined his head. "I could use another cup of coffee. And you promised me my just deserts. Unless you're too tired . . . ?"

He was giving her an out, she realized with surprise. And she *was* tired, though not as exhausted as she usually was at the end of the day.

The easiest, and safest, route would be to plead exhaustion and hightail it home before something happened. But knowing how much effort he'd put into making some sense of her wine cellar, Liss just couldn't bring herself to do it. Besides, she might find out something interesting about him if she didn't flee.

"I'll go put on a pot of coffee," she said, hoping she wasn't making one of those memorable mistakes she'd live to regret. "Come upstairs when you're ready."

In the silent kitchen, she took a deep calming breath. She was really going to have to stop having heart palpitations every time she looked at him, she scolded herself, or she could hardly blame him for trying to take advantage of the situation.

It was one thing to behave like a gentleman when a woman clearly indicated she wasn't interested. It was asking for a miracle, though, to expect a virile man not to respond to a woman who looked at him like a chocoholic who'd spied a box of Godivas.

Determined to regain control of the situation, Liss busied herself grinding fresh coffee beans. She had a small pot of coffee and two slices of chocolate amaretto cheesecake waiting at a small table in the dining room when Josh emerged from the cellar.

He approached her in silence.

"That looks like disapproval," she said lightly, wondering again why just the hint of his disapproval seemed to hit such a deep chord in her.

He raised his eyebrows. "I didn't realize I was that obvious."

"You aren't. It's not what you do and say. It's more

what you don't do and say." Almost as if he was used to, and adept at, keeping his thoughts and emotions to himself. "So, what's wrong?"

"What should I tackle first?"

"How about the table," she said, noticing the tiny cleft in his chin, "since that's what you looked at the longest."

Actually, Josh thought, he was pretty sure he'd looked at her the longest.

Unbelievably sexy and feminine in sandals and a simple white sundress, she'd set his heart thumping against his ribs the second he'd laid eyes on her that night. Even in the musty cellar, she'd been like a breath of fresh air and a strong dose of sunlight.

She was goodness and honesty personified. And he was a rat of the first order for lying to her.

"The table," she prompted, oblivious to the turmoil he was going through. "What's wrong with it?"

With effort Josh turned his attention to the table. "The sheet of Plexiglas. I realize that many restaurants use them and that there's nothing horribly wrong with them," he began, remembering her "give a pat on the back, then deliver the bad news" advice.

"But . . . ?" Liss prompted wryly.

"But they're inelegant."

Waiting for her reaction, Josh watched her look the table over carefully, her eyes avoiding his. "What do you suggest?"

Resisting the urge to tuck her blond hair behind her ear, which was bound to lead to a desire to touch her exquisitely soft throat, and then her small, equally irresistible breasts, Josh willed his body to behave itself.

"I'd suggest either getting rid of the Plexiglas," he

said, "or forget trying to strive for elegance and go casual."

"I'll take that under advisement." Still avoiding his gaze, Liss looked at the small wine bottle in his hand. "What's that?"

"A split of late-harvest Riesling to go with the cheesecake." He wondered how he could get her to look him in the eye, short of latching onto her and pulling her sweetly curved body against his. "It appears to be the only New York wine you have, and it's not on the wine list, so I thought you might not mind if we celebrated a little."

"What are we celebrating?"

"The fact that you haven't hit me over the head for my recalcitrance, what else?"

She shook her head at him. "We might need another reason for celebrating. The night's not over yet."

"I can't help myself. You're even easier to tease than my baby sister. Would you like to try the wine?"

She nodded. "What makes this a dessert wine? I thought Riesling was a dinner wine."

Pleased she was interested in learning, and trying not to think of all the things he'd like to teach her, Josh set down the two wineglasses he'd picked up in the kitchen. "It usually is. Late-harvest Riesling is made from carefully picked grapes that have been left on the vine past regular harvest time."

"They're sweeter?" Liss guessed.

He poured a small amount of the golden wine into the glasses and handed one to her. "Taste it."

Obediently lifting the glass to her mouth, Liss took a sip of the sweet nectar.

"Like it?" he asked.

"It's heavenly." She took another sip. "Why don't we have more of it?"

Josh sipped from his own glass. "That's what I was going to ask you. Did Ray pick out the original vintages you serve?"

"Of course. He knew a lot about wine. He was always looking for new ones to serve at the restaurant." She thought a moment. "Though I don't remember him ever being particularly interested in New York wines. He preferred European ones."

"Maybe this was one he meant to try and never got around to it." Josh sat down beside her. "I've been thinking."

"That's enough to get me worrying," Liss quipped. "What about?"

"Your cellar. Were you serious when you said you weren't selling much wine, or were you just trying to distract me?"

"I was serious. And I was trying to distract you."

He watched as she focused on her slice of cheesecake, then her glass of wine. Everywhere but at him.

Finally she glanced up at him. "Why are you looking at me like that?"

"I was trying to gauge your reaction, if you liked the way the wine goes with the cheesecake."

"Yes, I do," she answered, but she still looked as though she suspected something else was on his mind.

Josh took her hand. "Can I ask you something?"

Her expression changed from speculative to wary. "If you want."

"Why did you defend me tonight?"

She bit her lip. "You mean with Rob? You heard that?"

"Why did you do it?"

"I thought he was being unfair. It's not like you've stolen my silverware. . . ." She paused. "You haven't, have you?"

He tried not to smile with pleasure. "No."

"Don't let it go to your head," she admonished.

"I didn't." He kissed her wrist, his eyes on hers. "It went straight to my heart."

She tried to tug her hand free. "You must be easily impressed."

He wouldn't let her go. "Actually, I'm damned hard to impress. And even harder to maneuver."

"You think I maneuvered you?"

His smile was wry. "I think you're a lot more devious than you look. Certainly sneakier than I gave you credit for. Why did you have me do the inventory of the cellar?"

She shrugged. "Because I never have the time to do it myself. And because I don't know all that much about wine."

Josh played with her fingers. "I thought you were joking when you said all you knew was telling whites from reds. I guess this explains how you ended up with the Montepulciano d'Abruzzo."

"That was a mistake. I'll bet you never make mistakes."

"Oh, I make mistakes all right. Usually very large ones. Are you mad at me?" he asked when she didn't speak again.

"No," she said without hesitation. "I'm mad at myself."

"Why?"

"Because I sometimes have a lamentable habit of not looking before I leap."

"And you think you're in danger of leaping in the near future?"

"I think it might be a possibility."

"Ah."

She looked wary again. "What does 'ah' mean?"

"Nothing in particular." He stood up, helping her rise as well. "Anything else you'd like to know before we call it a night?"

He made his voice husky, seductive, hoping she might want to learn some very intimate things about him. Very personal things, preferably taught in the dark.

She cleared her throat, then disappointed him by saying, "Yes. What the devil is a Vino Nobile di Montepulciano, anyway?"

He hid his chagrin behind a smile. "It's a cousin of Chianti and Brunello. Any other questions?"

"Yes. Where did you learn so much about wine?"

"I've drunk my share in and out of restaurants."

"That's not an answer. I know a number of people who drink a lot of wine, and they're not connoisseurs, they're drunks."

"My dad owned a small winery," he admitted, knowing that not telling her would whet her curiosity further.

Actually, his father still owned and ran the winery, but if he told Liss that, she'd naturally want to know which one. And being the naturally nosy type, once she knew that she'd insist on going to see it.

When he'd taken her job offer, he'd had no idea how curious she'd turn out to be. And how hard it would be to continue lying to her. Or keeping his hands off her.

"You look deep in thought," he said, wondering if

she was beginning to put two and two together, and coming up with five. Wondering if he was going to be able to satisfy his craving for her with just a kiss. "What are you thinking?"

"I'm thinking you have hidden talents," she said, resting her hands on his forearms.

Determined to keep her mind, and her body if necessary, occupied and off that particular subject, Josh pulled her close, melding them together from the waist down. "I can do a number of things fairly well."

"Oh?"

"I kiss pretty good."

"You already demonstrated that."

"That wasn't a kiss. That was a sampling."

"Does that mean you're going to kiss me again?"

"Do you want me to?"

She hesitated. "What if I said no?"

"Are you saying no?"

"No."

"Is that yes, you're saying no?" He brushed his nose against hers. "Or no, you're saying yes?"

"It's no, I'm saying no," she said, her hands tightening on his arms. "But I think it should be yes, I'm saying yes."

He nodded solemnly. "I'm glad we've got that clarified." His arms slipped around her so easily, it was as if they'd always belonged there. "Let's see if we can clarify it even further."

And then he kissed her, and this time, even though it was a relatively short kiss, it was anything but sweet as he plundered her mouth, coaxing her soft lips apart into an openmouthed kiss that seared him down to his soul.

She clung to him, her body pressing against his as

his mouth left hers briefly, only to come back again. And again. And then again. Tasting her. Teasing her. Enticing her.

Finally she pulled away in protest. "Don't."

His breathing rough, he focused his gaze on her trembling mouth. "Why?"

"Because I want you to work for me," she said, "and I don't think it would be wise if we let our relationship get too personal."

He brushed his knuckles across her cheek. "What kind of job are you offering that would make it more lucrative than me kissing you? Inventorying the freezer?"

"No." She stepped back from him. "I was hoping you'd contact some of the local wineries. Expand our wine list so that we feature some New York wines. It seems silly not to, when they're made right here."

He let her move away, but it wasn't without effort. "And you want me to do it because you think I need an honest job? Or because I have some knowledge of wine?"

She managed an apologetic smile. "Both."

"You wouldn't also be trying to find me a job that takes me out of the restaurant because you think I'm getting too personal, would you?"

She looked at him with wide eyes. "Would I do that?"

"I don't know. Would you?"

"You were the one who inventoried the wine cellar and decided it's come up wanting. I'm just asking you to complete the job. Does the idea interest you?"

Josh studied her flushed face, trying not to look at her mouth. The job didn't interest him half as much as she did. She was sweet when he expected her to be devious. And devious when he expected her to be sweet. The truth was, he wanted to get to know her better. A lot better. He wanted to rip off her clothes and make hot passionate love to her.

The problem was, of course, when she eventually discovered who he really was—and she would, sooner rather than later if he didn't keep his distance—he didn't think she would ever forgive him.

The wisest course of action would be to sever their relationship now, before he hurt her. Before he ended up making love to her. Because if he kept on seeing her, that was what was going to happen.

She was as attracted to him as he was to her. He knew it, even if she didn't. A decent man—and he liked to think he fell into that category—would do her a favor and get the hell out of her life.

"I'll think about the job," he said, having no intention whatsoever of doing anything of the kind.

SIX

The knock on her front door came at just after nine on Sunday. Gritting her teeth, because, in true Murphy's Law fashion, she was just about to step into the shower, Liss muttered a pithy oath as the pounding grew loud enough to wake someone halfway across the country.

Yanking on a terry-cloth robe, she stomped to the front door. She threw it open, ready to bite off the head of the perpetrator.

"Good morning, Liss. Have a good night?"

Liss stared at the handsome smiling face of her newest, and definitely most exasperating, employee. "What I was about to have was a shower. What the devil are you doing here?"

She'd spent half the night thinking about Josh Farrington in various stages of undress, with her, and it was almost as if her inability to get him off her mind had conjured him out of thin air.

He smiled at her. "I came to pick you up, of course."

Liss pulled her robe closer around her. "Pick me up to go where?" The Lakeview was closed on Sundays and Mondays, and as far as she could remember, she had nothing planned for the day. Especially not with Josh Farrington.

How a man could look so sexy on a Sunday morning was beyond her, but he was. Clean-shaven and impossibly attractive in a white shirt, khaki slacks, and boat shoes that looked as comfortable as an old friendship, there was nothing threatening about him at all. Still, Liss felt nervous just looking at him.

"I'm picking you up," he said patiently, "so we can scout out what the local wineries have to offer. You haven't forgotten, have you?"

She frowned in confusion. "I wasn't planning on going with you." On the contrary, she'd planned the excursion to get him as far away from the Lakeview, and her, as she could manage.

"Why not?"

She put her hands on her hips. "Because I don't know that much about New York wines, that's why not."

Besides that, she'd thought up the task for *him* in particular, not only because it seemed the perfect job for someone with wine knowledge and no current job, but because she could employ him yet still not have to be around him. Consequently, she wouldn't have to worry about getting any more involved with him. He'd clearly figured that out and was determined to ignore her maneuvering.

"If you don't know much about New York wine," he said, sounding annoyingly reasonable, "then it's about high time you learn, don't you think?"

What she thought was that he was turning out to

be an even bigger problem than she'd first suspected. Another reason she'd offered him the job of evaluating, then expanding, her wine selection was that she'd hoped he'd develop some connections with the local wineries, which might lead to a better, and more permanent, job.

But if he insisted she go with him, she was fairly sure the day wouldn't end with just a stolen kiss or two. And all her good intentions would be for naught. . . .

Liss blinked at him. "I thought you were going to think about taking the job and let me know."

"I thought about it and decided I couldn't say no. Well?"

She tried to think of a way to get rid of him while she could still think clearly. "Well, what?"

"Aren't you going to invite me in?"

"I haven't decided yet," she said. Inviting him into her living room was the last thing she wanted to do. Who knew what would happen? "How did you know where I live?"

"I followed you home last night."

She frowned. "That was a sneaky thing to do."

"Would you have given me your address if I'd asked?"

"No."

He smiled in satisfaction. "I rest my case."

"What do you think you're doing?" she demanded as he gently pushed her out of the way and walked past her. Seating himself on the arm of her dark blue couch, he looked about as immovable as the Rock of Gibraltar.

"I told you. I need you to go with me to pick out some wine. I'm not going alone," he informed her even while she was thinking of believable excuses, and not so believable excuses, why she couldn't go with him. "So you might as well save your breath. Not that I don't like you breathless, mind you. I'd just prefer it came from kissing, not talking." He smiled as Liss fervently tried not to think about kissing him. And about how warm his lips had felt the night before . . .

She shook her head. "I'm not going with you. I offered *you* the job."

"So you did." He smiled. "Unfortunately, unless you give me access to your checking account or one of your credit cards, I don't have anything to buy the wine with. I'm broke, remember? You'd better get dressed," he added while she fumed in frustrated silence. They both knew she had no intention of giving him access to her money. "If I take you along with you in your nightie, people are bound to start wondering exactly what kind of a relationship we have."

Liss was wondering herself what kind of a relationship they had. "I was heading for the shower," she said grumpily.

He settled himself more comfortably on the sofa. "No problem. I'm in no hurry. I'll wait."

Liss hesitated. Then, recognizing that he wasn't going to leave without her, she headed for the bathroom. Locking the door, she leaned against it for a moment, desperately thinking about what to do.

On one level, she knew he was right. She really did need to become better versed in New York wine so she wouldn't be dependent on him, or anyone else, to pick what the Lakeview served.

On another level, a more emotional one, she knew that if they spent the whole day together, by evening's end she was likely to be emotionally, if not physically, entangled with him.

"I'm going to give you until the count of ten," Josh announced through the door, "and then, if you haven't at least started the shower, I'm coming in to help you get dressed."

Muttering nasty remarks about high-handed men, Liss turned on the tap. She stepped into the steamy, hot shower and took her sweet time washing her body and her hair. Then, getting out again, she leisurely toweled off and blow-dried her hair. She took an extra ten minutes applying her lipstick before she got dressed, as slowly as she could, then emerged to find Josh standing in her small living room, examining her collection of miniature animals.

He turned as she stopped in the doorway, disgruntled to find him still there. "Nice collection," he said. "Have any foxes?"

"Yes," she said, sliding on a pair of sandals. "There's one standing in my living room at the moment."

He sighed in satisfaction. "I love reasonable women."

"You wouldn't know reasonable," she retorted, "if it came up and bit you."

"You're just grumpy because you haven't had any breakfast yet. How about some cappuccino and croissants?"

She stared as he walked, then followed him out onto her sunny brick patio. "What is this?" she asked, her voice riddled with suspicion, as she followed him.

"Breakfast. I wasn't sure what you'd have on hand, so I brought something along." Josh pulled out a chair for her. "Have a seat."

Liss sat on the white patio chair, eyeing him with distrust.

"You know," he said as he dished her out a bowl of sliced strawberries, "you really shouldn't skip breakfast like you do. Didn't your mother ever tell you that it's the most important meal of the day?"

"My mother never ate breakfast. She was always on a diet. What makes you think I skip breakfast?"

"Anthony told me." Josh handed her a cup of cappuccino, dusted with chocolate. "He said you worked too much and ate too little. And also that you worry too much."

"I think he talks too much." Not at all sure she liked being the object of Josh's curiosity, Liss sat back and tasted the cappuccino. "Did you ask my other employees about me as well?"

"Sure. Mary Lee was a fount of information."

Liss frowned at him over the flowered cup. "What could she possibly have told you? She's only worked for me a little over a week."

Josh poured orange juice. "She said you were the nicest person she'd ever met. Personally I would've also said you were kind and generous and attractive as well. How's your cappuccino?"

"It's wonderful," Liss said truthfully, blushing at the compliment. "Where did you learn how to use a cappuccino maker?"

"It doesn't exactly take a rocket scientist to run one. It just takes a little patience. Can I ask you something?"

Liss feigned shock. "You mean there's something my employees didn't tell you about me?"

"There's probably a thing or two I still don't know about you," he allowed. "Though I'm working on it."

Knowing she shouldn't be surprised by his interest, since she'd been doing her best to find out everything she could about him, Liss shrugged. "What do
you want to know?"

"How come you don't serve cappuccino at the
Lakeview?"

Puzzled by the question, Liss put down her cup
and spooned up a strawberry. "Who says I don't?"

"Mary Lee."

Liss sighed in exasperation. "Lord. We have the
machine. It's just that I'm the only one who's managed to figure out how to get the milk to foam. I keep
trying to teach Rob and Annie, one of my other waitresses, but they can't seem to get the hang of it."

"And you couldn't make it the other night because
you were busy cooking." Josh nodded in understanding as he spread a yellow napkin onto his lap. "So why
did you buy such a complicated machine? There are
others on the market that are much easier to use."

Liss paused before answering. "I didn't buy it. Ray
did."

Josh looked at her in thoughtful silence as he
stirred sugar into his cappuccino. "I imagine it hasn't
been easy to run the restaurant since he died."

Refusing to feel sorry for herself, Liss shrugged
again. "I do the best I can. Where did you get the
croissants?"

Josh's smile was teasing. "Wegman's, where else?
Would you prefer chocolate-filled or almond-filled?"

"Chocolate, please."

Josh passed it to her. "You're a true chocoholic,
aren't you?"

She bit into the flaky pastry, savoring the creamy
chocolate filling. "Who told you that? Anthony?"

"No one had to tell me. More than half of the desserts on the Lakeview's menu are chocolate."

"It's terrible to be so predictable." She licked a sticky finger. "How come you're being so nice, bringing me breakfast?"

"I'm a nice man."

"Yes," she said, feeling giddy as her eyes met his. "I believe you are."

She hadn't thought he was going to be when she'd first met him. She'd thought he looked self-centered and self-satisfied. But in this instance, familiarity hadn't bred contempt. It had fostered something else entirely.

"There's no need to sound so surprised," he said.

"I can't help it," she confessed. "You never seem to do what I expect you to. You're very difficult to figure out, you know that?"

He refilled her glass of orange juice. "So are you."

"Me?" Her eyebrows rose. "How?"

Josh's voice was filled with bemusement. "Sometimes you seem so innocent and naive. Like the way you hire help. Few people would put up with Mary Lee's lack of grace or Anthony's being so erratic. But there are times I think you're not gullible at all."

Praying he was right, Liss said hopefully, "I'm not?"

"How much of what I told you last night about wine did you already know?" he asked instead.

Liss just looked at him.

"You played dumb to find out how much I knew, didn't you?"

She finished her croissant and wiped her fingers on a napkin. "Why would I do that?"

"I imagine for the same reason you've kept on

Mary Lee and Anthony, despite their flaws. Because you're determined to help them make something of themselves."

"I really don't know all that much about New York wines," she said, refusing to look at him. Or, she admitted silently, all that much about how to handle a man like him.

"I believe you," he said. "That's why you're coming with me today." Finishing his own croissant, Josh rose and began stacking the dishes. "Stay put," he ordered as Liss started to rise to help.

"I can't just sit here while you work," she protested, picking up a dish.

He took it out of her hands. "Why not?"

"Because I can't." She gathered up the basket that had held the croissants. "That's why not."

Josh took the basket from her. "You mean you're a workaholic. Go sit in the living room while I clean up here, if you can't stand watching me work while you rest."

"I'd rather help."

"I'd rather make love than work," Josh told her as he headed into the kitchen. "So if you're still here when I come out again . . ."

Fairly sure he meant it, Liss shot his retreating back a deadly look, then turned back to the living room. A few minutes later, having cleared the table and rinsed the dishes, Josh joined her.

"You look like the cat who's swallowed the canary," she said as he surveyed the room.

"Do I? I was thinking what an interesting picture this is."

She watched as he walked over to her fireplace to get a closer look at the picture on the wall above it.

"I like impressionistic paintings," she said, expect-ing criticism for her taste in art, which Ray had de-nounced as "feminine."

"Yes." Josh glanced at the two smaller paintings near the front door. "I can see that. Who did them?"

"I had a waiter who worked for me, right after Ray died, who was an art student."

"And he needed money for college."

Liss hesitated. "Yes."

"So you bought the paintings from him to help finance his education."

"They're nice paintings," she said in her own de-fense, surprised he'd come to the right conclusion so quickly.

Josh turned to look at her. "You know, Mary Lee's right about you. You're a nice woman."

"You mean predictable and boring."

"Sweetheart, you're anything but predictable. And the last word I'd use to describe you is boring." His uncharacteristically bland smile made even her toe-nails sit up and take notice. "So, are you going to be reasonable about coming with me?"

Giving in, she picked up her purse from the coffee table and checked to see if she had her house keys and checkbook with her. "Do I have a choice?"

"About going with me? Not really. It's your res-taurant. You at least ought to have a say in what wine you serve, whether you want a say or not. But I'll let you drive half the time, if it makes you feel any less threatened as a feminist."

"Half the time nothing," Liss told him as she walked ahead of him out the door. "If I'm going, I'm driving. All the time." As she approached his racy black Corvette she held out her hand for the keys.

"You're planning on driving my car?" he asked, looking just as appalled by the idea as she thought he would.

"What's the matter?" she asked. "Don't you trust me?"

"Considering your present mood, I'm not sure. Are you always this testy in the morning?"

"I'm not testy. I'm being assertive."

"What's the difference between being testy and assertive?"

"When a woman is being assertive," Liss explained, "she resists the urge to whap a man over the head when he shows up unexpectedly on a Sunday morning and insists on bossing her around."

"You think I'm bossing you around?"

"Did you *ask* me if I'd come with you today? Or did you tell me?"

Josh surveyed her for a moment, taking in her freshly washed blond hair, her pretty face sans makeup, except for lipstick, and her pale pink sundress. And he found himself jamming his fists into the pockets of his slacks so he didn't pull her into his arms and kiss her until she was mindless.

She was right. He'd been bossy. Mostly because he'd anticipated her resistance.

Unable to stay away from her, he hadn't given her a chance to decide on her own to come with him, because he'd been fairly sure she wouldn't want to. And he knew why. She was fighting her growing attraction for him, the same way he was trying to keep his paws off her.

Amused at the way she could hold her own with him, he asked, "Is this, by any chance, another lesson in etiquette?"

She shrugged. "As long as we're learning things today, I don't see why we ought to avoid a few pointers on male-female relationships. And you have yet to pass over your car keys."

He reluctantly dug them out of his pocket, but held on to them for a moment more. "Don't you want to know where we're going?"

She walked over to the Corvette and opened the driver's door. "I figured we'd head down highway fourteen and hit Fox Run and Anthony Road. Then I'd like to catch Wiemer's, Glenora, and Lakewood."

"Do you know the way?" he asked, still not getting into the car. "Because if you don't, I'm familiar with the area. . . ."

She looked at him in amusement. "I grew up in Rochester, and spent almost every summer on Seneca Lake. My folks had a cottage down at Kashong. Are you going to let me drive or not?"

It was a test, Josh knew, not unlike his "Farr test," and he was about to flunk it. Recognizing that letting her drive his treasured Corvette was important to their developing relationship, he reluctantly passed over the keys.

SEVEN

In spite of his good intentions as he relinquished control of his car, Josh still couldn't help backseat driving.

Giving Liss a list of instructions on how to get the car into reverse, and familiarizing her with the car's quirks, he stopped in midsentence when she hit the brakes halfway out of her driveway and turned to him.

"You know, this is probably going to come as a big shock to you, but I know how to drive. I've been driving since I was sixteen."

Josh found himself focusing on her mouth. "How old are you now?"

"Old enough not to answer that question just because someone feels like asking it." She glanced at him as she finished backing out of her graveled driveway. "How old are you?"

Josh tried not to cringe as she pressed hard on the gas pedal and the car's tires screeched around the first corner. "Old enough not to want to get into an accident."

"You *are* an accident," Liss told him, slowing down to a sedate twenty-five for the next curve.

"Really?" He gave her a speculative look. "What kind?"

"A head-on crash, impossible to avoid. Sit back and relax. I'm not going to hurt your precious car. I'm a very good driver."

"You're driving too fast."

"If anyone knows anything about moving too fast," she said, slowing down and driving like a little old lady, "it's you. You *are* going to behave yourself today, aren't you?"

"What do you think?"

"I think I'm going to hold your car keys as ransom, just in case you decide to try any funny stuff."

"What do you consider funny stuff?"

She just rolled her eyes and kept on driving, while Josh proceeded to close his own eyes and give a very good impression of praying. He didn't open them again until Liss pulled into the parking lot of the first winery and shut off the engine.

"If you cross yourself like that one more time," she said, "I swear I'm going to bop you one. What now?"

Josh exited the low-slung car. Coming around to the driver's side, he opened her door for her and helped her out. "I thought we'd try a few wines, to see if we like the winemaker's style."

"And if we do?"

"If we do, we pick out a few bottles and take them with us to try them in more depth later. Okay?"

"Whatever you say," Liss said dryly, since he'd been ordering her around all morning.

Obedient to the point of obsequiousness, just to

exasperate him the way he exasperated her, Liss didn't argue when Josh suggested they avoid the winery tour and head straight for the tasting room.

"Hi, folks." The young hostess behind the oak counter gave Liss a quick smile, then let her attention linger on Josh. "What would you like to try today?"

Josh looked at Liss, who shrugged. "How about the Cayuga white?" she said.

After two glasses had been poured, Liss lifted hers and gave Josh a questioning look. "What, exactly, are we looking for?"

"Besides good balance and a pleasant taste? Something that would make a good house wine."

"You mean one that's served by the glass?" She watched Josh concentrate on the aroma from his glass. "Why?"

"Because I think I've figured out why you sell so little wine." He tipped his glass to catch the light, checking for color and clarity. "You don't offer much in the way of a moderately priced wine. Even with your former kleptomaniac employee, most of what is in your cellar is expensive. There's virtually nothing there that sells for less than twenty-five dollars a bottle."

Liss sipped the chilled dry white wine, trying to keep an open mind as she listened. "You're right. Maybe I should stock some cheaper ones. Anything else?"

"You also don't offer any splits," he said as she checked her own glass for color. "It's not your fault. The industry hasn't exactly been responsive in that regard. But not everyone wants to order a whole bottle of wine when they know they're going to be driving home within the hour."

"And you think a house wine will solve both problems?"

"At least if you offer a house red and a house white, it'll give more people a choice of what they'd like to drink, and how much they'd like to drink. Do you like the Cayuga?"

She nodded. "I think it has possibilities. But I'd like to try a Melody, as well."

Josh looked at her a moment. "They don't offer it here. We'll have to hit Wagner's for that one. Where did you hear about Melody? It's not all that well-known."

She flushed. "I read a few of Ray's wine books last night. I thought it might be a good idea to know more about wine in general, and New York ones in particular. Are we going to try anything else?"

"How about a Ravat?"

As they progressed to the next wine Josh watched her tilt her glass to the side. "What do you think?" he asked.

"Great body," she said.

"I couldn't agree more. What else?"

"Nice legs," she said, referring to the viscosity and the way the wine lingered on the glass after it was swirled.

He nodded. "Great ones, I'd say."

"Are we still talking about wine?" she asked as blood suffused her cheeks.

Josh looked innocent. "What else would we be talking about? I think I'd prefer a higher sugar content and less alcohol in this one. It's up around thirteen percent. How about you?"

"I don't know anything about sugar or alcohol content," she confessed.

It was all the priming Josh needed. He insisted on teaching her all about sugar and alcohol, and about other subtleties to look for in a wine, so that she'd be better informed when she picked wines out in the future.

"Who's teaching who a trade here?" Liss wondered out loud as they drove to the next winery, with Liss at the wheel.

"You can't run a restaurant well if you don't know about every aspect of it," Josh said. "Wine is an important part of meal service. You do want to be independent, don't you?"

"Yes," Liss said, staring at him with new eyes. "I do."

But she was floored that he wanted her to be. Ray had always liked her to be slightly dependent on him, had more or less expected her to go along with decisions he made, without consulting her, or asking whether she agreed with him. That had made it all the harder when he'd died and she'd had to take over running the restaurant barely three months after they'd opened.

She hadn't been prepared for it. She'd made any number of horrible mistakes during the first few weeks and still had a lamentable habit of making rash decisions, especially when it involved people. Goodness knew, she was ready to leap into Josh Farrington's arms despite second, and third, thoughts.

"Why are you looking at me like that?" he asked.

"Because I think I'm seeing the real you."

And she liked what she saw. He wasn't the least bit threatened by her independence, she realized. In fact, he seemed to be determined to foster it.

His smile was wry. "Something tells me that isn't

going to keep you from teasing personal information out of me every chance you get." He frowned as he scanned the road ahead. "Pull over to the right shoulder. Looks like the car ahead is in trouble."

Surprised by his request, Liss pulled the Corvette off the road and parked behind a small Toyota with its hood up. "You can stay here if you like," Josh said, opening his door, "while I see what's wrong. I'll only be a minute."

Deciding to stay put, Liss watched Josh through the windshield as he walked up to the Toyota and began talking to the driver, who was standing in front of the opened hood, looking distinctly unhappy. After a moment Josh leaned over the engine. Liss couldn't see what he was doing, but after another minute the other men reentered his car. Liss heard the engine start.

She realized belatedly she should use the opportunity of Josh's absence to visually search the inside of the Corvette for clues about the man's habits and background.

Fortunately, he was out of the car long enough for her to do a thorough inspection. Unfortunately, the interior of the car was immaculate, with nary a wadded-up gum wrapper on the floor.

Exasperated, Liss looked up just in time to see that Josh had slammed the Toyota's hood shut and was talking to the driver. It was clear to Liss that the driver was trying to hand Josh some money. It was equally clear that Josh had no intention of taking it.

After a minute the other man shook Josh's hand, then drove off.

"Why did you do that?" Liss asked as Josh

climbed back into the car beside her. "To impress me?"

He plucked a tissue from the box between the front seats and wiped engine oil off his fingers. "I did it because he needed help." He glanced over at her. "Wouldn't you have done the same?"

She nodded. "Yes." But she hadn't expected him to. She'd thought his helping Mary Lee had been more to boost his standing in her eyes than it had been to aid her inexperienced waitress. But now she was beginning to realize that Josh Farrington helped those in need because that was the kind of man he was. The kind of man you could admire. The kind of man you could fall in love with.

Liss cleared her throat. "What did you do, anyway?"

"One of the wires had come loose inside the distributor cap. I reattached it. What does that look mean?"

"Nothing. I was just wondering if you were a car mechanic at some point in your life." Liss put the Corvette in gear.

"It's not something I've ever made a living at, if that's what you're asking. I used to be something of a hot-rodder when I was a teenager. I picked up a bit about car mechanics along the way."

Not really surprised, since his hands seemed to indicate that he had held white-collar jobs, Liss nodded. "Do you think you could teach me something about car engines so I don't get stranded some snowy night in the middle of December?"

"If you like."

She felt his gaze on her as she drove. "Why are you looking at me like that?"

"Because I like what I see. You really don't like being dependent on anyone else for anything, do you?"

"I don't like being helpless," she said. "Or out of control."

"Sometimes," Josh said, his voice low, "it's hard to always be in control of things."

You're telling me, Liss thought as she felt her pulse rate careening out of control. With only the slightest encouragement from him, she knew she would stop the car and let him pull her into his arms. Would willingly deepen their relationship beyond mere friendship.

Afraid to let that happen, she smiled brightly. "So, what now? Shall we help the nearest farmer plow his fields?"

Josh took a moment to answer. "You know, if I didn't know you better, I'd think you were being sassy to hide the fact that you're beginning to like me, and you don't think you should."

"I'm not being sassy," Liss said, ignoring the rest of his statement. "I'm being—"

"Assertive." He finished her sentence for her. "So how about you assertively pull in at the next driveway." He pointed to a narrow driveway fifty feet ahead. "There's a new place that's just opened. Could be interesting."

"What's the plan of action?" Liss asked as they came into sight of the Tudor-style building.

"Same as before. We try some reds and some whites."

"I'm not sure I should drink anymore and drive," Liss said, looking for an excuse to put some physical distance between them. "Maybe I should just stay in the car this time."

He shook his head. "I need your help."

"No, you don't."

He cupped her chin, forcing her to look at him. "Yes, I do. You're going to give the woman's perspective on what we try. I'll give the male."

Liss took a calming breath. "They're different?"

His quick smile was thoroughly male, and thoroughly wicked. "You haven't noticed that men and women are different?"

She flushed. "I didn't realize they were different when it came to wine."

"Well, they are."

"How?"

"Women invariably go for white wine. Men usually prefer red."

"Why?"

"I don't know why. Difference in taste buds, I imagine."

"Or a perception that white wine has fewer calories." She carefully removed his hand from her face while she still had the presence of mind to do it.

Josh looked like he wanted to reinitiate contact, but he kept his hands to himself. "It's important to know your clientele. What they like and don't like."

Always on the lookout for a clue about his identity, Liss immediately perked up. "You're sure you've never run a restaurant before?"

He shook his head at her persistence. "This is just common sense. You study who your customers are, what they like to eat and drink, and you provide it."

It made sense to Liss. If only she could decipher the man sitting next to her. She couldn't figure out how they seemed so different, yet appeared to have so much in common. She also couldn't figure out how they'd become more than just employer and employee so swiftly.

But they had. And she didn't know what to do about it.

Fifteen wines later she still didn't know what to do about it. Or what to do about him. He simply refused to let her be impersonal.

Liss pondered the situation as she stood under the grapevine trellis on the patio at the last winery of the day. She was waiting for Josh to load their purchases into the Corvette. The weather was sunny and warm, and though there were a few dark clouds in the distance, the view of the deep blue waters of Seneca Lake stretching out below was breathtaking.

"This is so beautiful," she said as Josh joined her.

"It is, isn't it? Too bad the Lakeview doesn't have an outdoor deck or patio since it's right on the lake. There's a terrific view. But no one gets to enjoy it."

She sighed. "I know. It's one of the things that Ray wanted to do. He was even going to build the deck himself to save money. But he never got a chance to do it." She turned to Josh with hopeful eyes. "I don't suppose you know anything about carpentry?"

"I can tell a nail from a hammer," he said. "That's about it."

"You fixed the cellar steps," she pointed out.

"That was desperation, not skill, at work. I was afraid that one, or both, of us would trip and break a leg." He paused for effect. "Not that I wouldn't like you prone, of course . . ."

She was likely to be prone if she didn't get something in her stomach besides wine, Liss thought, feel-

•

ing too dizzy to stand, let alone drive. And not at all capable of resisting Josh.

He'd more or less behaved himself all day, giving her no more than a touch on the arm here, a lingering look there. . . . But she didn't think his goodness would last.

And, quite frankly, she wasn't sure hers was going to, either.

The longer she was with him, the harder she found it to remember that she still knew virtually nothing about him. That she shouldn't get involved with him.

The problem was, she was involved with him already. She was in right up to her eyeballs. Whether he realized it or not, spending this day with him had made it that much more obvious to her. She was falling head over heels in love with him. Good or bad, it was happening. And there didn't seem to be a blessed thing she could do about it.

"You need to get some food into you," he said, apparently aware of how light-headed she was feeling. "Why don't you relax while I pick up a few things? They carry some cheese and fruit and crackers in the wine shop. We can have a picnic before we head back."

Liss agreed and headed for the ladies' room to get herself in order as Josh went to buy them some food.

Ten minutes later she emerged to find Josh leaning against the patio railing, looking out across the lake. He straightened as she approached.

"I'm sorry." She smiled in apology. "I needed to sober up. I think I drank when I should've sipped. Have you been waiting for me long?"

Sometimes, Josh thought, he felt as if he'd been

waiting for her all his life. She was turning out to be everything he'd ever wanted in a woman. Honest. Forthright. Generous and giving. Not to mention wonderfully sexy, even though she didn't realize it.

The more he was with her, the more he wanted to be with her.

Which made the current situation that much more difficult. He was getting increasingly uncomfortable with the role he was playing. He'd been feeling pangs of guilt all day as he thought about how he was fooling her. He knew damned well he needed to come clean. He'd known from day one.

But, being all too human, he kept putting off telling Liss who he was because he didn't know how to do it without wrecking his relationship with her. He was, after all, the one person in the world she was most likely to despise.

Part of the reason he'd wanted her to come along that day was so that he could work up to telling her the truth. He'd lied to her, and deep down he knew that the one thing she'd hate was deception. The longer the deception, he figured, the deeper the hate. And the less likely it would be that she'd forgive him.

She was way too trusting. After all, she'd taken him at face value. Well, maybe not totally. She'd been doing her best to weasel information out of him, just as he'd been doing his best to keep it from her. She'd still gone and hired him, though.

Lord knew, he wanted to tell her the truth and get it over with. But he didn't want to disillusion her. And he didn't want to lose her. Didn't even want to *think* about losing her.

Pushing the thought away before it could take root and grow, Josh shrugged. "I'm in no hurry." As she swayed against him he studied her flushed face with sudden concern. "Are you okay?"

She looked up at him, embarrassed. "I don't usually sip wine before lunch."

"Point taken. As much as I love the idea of you swooning into my arms"—he linked his long fingers with hers—"I think we'd better go have something to eat."

EIGHT

Josh escorted her to the car, guided her inside, then drove them to a grassy hill overlooking the lake.

"Are you sure this is okay?" Liss asked as he helped her out. "I mean, we're not going to be arrested for trespassing or anything?"

"We're fine. As long as we don't steal any grapes from the vines nearby, the owner isn't likely to mind." He handed her a canvas tote bag filled with food. "You're not turning into a worrywart on me, are you?"

"Anyone would turn into a worrywart if they were around you long enough. After all that complaining about my driving, do you realize you never went under sixty the whole way here?"

"I didn't think you noticed the speedometer, you being half-inebriated and all."

"I'm not inebriated," she informed him loftily. "I'm slightly unfocused."

"If you say so." Smiling, Josh grabbed a plaid blanket from the car and arranged it on the ground.

As Liss dropped down on it before her legs gave out, Josh sat beside her. He dug into the tote bag and laid out an impressive array of cheese, potted meats, crackers, bread, and fruit.

Liss stared at the delicacies in amazement. "You got all that while I was throwing cold water on my face?"

"I'm a quick shopper."

"A quick talker too," she murmured as he passed her a stone-ground wheat cracker loaded with Brie. "Exactly how did you get that discount on the case of wine?"

Josh popped a grape into his mouth. "All the wineries will give you a case discount if you ask." He handed her another cracker with deviled ham on it. "What did you think of the last wine we tried?"

"The red one?" Liss pondered the question a moment. "I thought it was like drinking Drāno. The finish wash awful. Uh, was awful."

Shaking his head in mocking disapproval, Josh passed her another cracker with cheese. "De Chaunacs have never been my personal favorite. Too much color, not enough character. Are you always this tipsy after just a sip or two of wine?"

"I've been drinking wine all day," Liss protested as he handed her a plastic cup filled with lemon-flavored springwater.

"You were supposed to take a sip of wine," he said, stretching out and resting on one elbow, "then eat a cracker to cleanse your palate. Otherwise the results are skewed. And you get drunk."

"Is this going to be another lesson?" she asked. "Because if it is, I think this time I'd better take notes."

Even though he told himself only a clod would take advantage of her when she wasn't quite sober, Josh couldn't help thinking of some of the things he'd like to teach her. Like how to open her mouth more when he kissed her. He wanted to kiss her again. Not just a quick peck this time, stolen before she could protest. He wanted to kiss her thoroughly and deeply, until her cheeks were flushed and her gray eyes were glazed with wanting. . . .

"I don't think you should do that," she said as he absently stroked the soft skin on the inside of her wrist with his thumb.

"Why not? Don't you like it?"

"This is interesting cheese," she said, rather obviously changing the subject. "What is it?"

"It's Havarti with dill. A friend introduced me to it."

"A man friend?" she asked. "Or a woman friend?"

"A woman friend. Jealous?"

"No. Yes." Liss sighed. "I'm not sure."

"I think we may be making progress here." He traced the light veins on her wrist.

Liss took a deep breath and let it out again. "I'm not sure I'd call this progress."

"What would you call it?"

"Trouble."

His mouth curved into a wry smile. "I thought that's what you called me."

"It is."

"You wouldn't if you'd known me longer. I'm really a very normal, very reliable guy." He picked up her hand, tracing the lines in her palm. "Where did you meet Ray?"

Obviously surprised by the question, Liss hesitated

before answering. "He was head chef at the restaurant where I was pastry chef. Mutual friends convinced us to double-date, and the rest, as they say, is history."

"Do you still see the friends you had when you were married?" Josh asked, wanting to know if she had a social life, though he suspected she didn't.

"No." Her attempt at a smile made him want to hold her, to comfort her.

Still touching her hand, Josh leaned back on both elbows so he could watch her face without being too close. "Why not?"

She lifted a shoulder. "It's a funny thing about married friends. Once you aren't married anymore, they don't seem to know what to do or say. After a while they stop trying."

Josh nodded. It had been the same for him. His married friends had tried, in the beginning, to match him up with some single female friend or other. Later they'd stopped calling altogether.

"Do you have family in New York City?" she asked.

"No." He didn't add that he could see his folks' house from where they sat.

"What about your sister?"

"What sister?"

"The one who's apparently as easy to tease as me."

He grinned. "You don't miss much, do you? My younger sister lives in L.A. so she can have fun in the sun. She hates snow."

"And your folks?"

"They like snow okay." He chuckled at Liss's look of reprimand. "They own a small business. What about you?" he asked, aware of every flicker of emotion in her eyes. "Do you have family around here?"

She shook her head. "Just Rob. He's like a brother to me."

Josh laced his fingers together so he wouldn't reach out and touch the silky strands of gold brushing her cheeks. "Where are your parents? How come they don't help out with the restaurant?"

"Because they're in Alaska." She took a sip of water. "They try to send money now and then. I always say no."

"Why?"

"Because I'm not a child, that's why." She passed him the basket of fruit. "My parents shouldn't have to support me."

"No brothers or sisters?"

"No. How about you? Any brothers?"

"You're awfully nosy," he complained.

Liss slathered more Brie on a cracker. "Look who's talking. Has anyone ever told you that you have a lamentable habit of asking lots of questions, but volunteer very little information about yourself?"

He peeled the fur off a kiwi. "You want to know more about me?"

"Yes."

"Why?"

Liss hesitated. "Because I find you interesting. Because you work for me." Because she thought she was falling in love with him.

"In that order?"

"That's for me to know. I'd like to make a deal with you."

"What kind of deal?"

Liss looked him straight in the eye. "For every question you ask me, you have to give me at least one tidbit of information about yourself. It can be as small or as large as you like, but it has to be specific and not general. For instance, if you say you like cars, or art, or fruit, you have to indicate what kind. Deal?"

To her surprise, he thought a moment, then nodded. "Deal. What kinds of things do you want to know?"

"That counted as a question," she informed him. "My answer is that I'll settle, for the moment, with very basic stuff. Like, what's your middle name?"

Josh just looked at her. She considered it an innocuous question, but his apparent reluctance in answering it sent her curiosity soaring. She started to speak again, but he forestalled her.

"Don't you want to know something a little more interesting, like where was I born? Or what sign I am?"

She gave him a sunny smile. "You now owe me two more pieces of personal information."

"Don't you think you're being a little literal here?"

She batted her lashes at him. "Three more pieces. I'm doing you a favor, you know," she said as he eyed her with feigned menace. "If nothing else I'll probably break this awful habit of yours of asking questions all the time."

"What makes you think I won't try to get even?"

"I'll tell you anything about me you want to know," she said. "As long as you don't start getting too personal. And that was—"

"Four," he finished for her. His deep brown eyes glittered as he contemplated her. Finally he said, "I was born just outside of Syracuse. Went to public schools and had a disgustingly normal childhood. I like old sports cars that have been restored, French

Impressionist art, every fruit I've ever met. And sassy women."

Liss was stunned by this sudden volley of revelations. Attempting to keep the conversation flowing, and without thinking about the consequences, she asked, "How do you feel about sassy women employers?"

"Why don't I just show you?"

He said it so innocently, she didn't realize what he intended to do until she was lying beneath him in the soft grass. She stared up at him, surprised, wary. Excited.

"What are you doing?" she croaked, her throat suddenly dry as parchment.

"I'm not *doing* anything. But I'm *planning* on kissing you."

He didn't move, though. And the fact that he didn't, merely kept his mouth so close to hers that Liss had to lower her lashes to keep from staring him in the eye, made her aware of his longer, stronger body on top of hers. The firm feel of his muscled thighs on hers. The evidence of his desire pressing into her.

"What if I don't want you to kiss me?" she asked, reveling in the warmth of him as he linked his fingers with hers, holding her arms down.

"Has anyone ever told you that you ask too many questions?"

"Yes. You have. About every time I ask one. This isn't your way of getting even, is it?" Liss asked. His lips were so close to hers, all she had to do was lift her head maybe a millimeter or so, and their mouths would touch.

He seemed to realize that too.

"Actually"—his lips brushed hers, inciting every cell in her body to riot—"it's my way of telling you I want to get to know you better."

Liss took a deep breath to relieve the constriction in her lungs, and felt her breasts press against his hard chest. "How much better?"

Letting go of one hand, he smoothed her hair off her face, as if he couldn't keep from touching her. "In a lot more depth than most employer-employee relationships allow."

"Oh," Liss said, feeling her blood pulsing through her veins.

"Oh, indeed." He kissed the corner of her mouth.

A spiral of warmth coiled deep inside her. "Does this mean I should discourage you? Or fire you?"

He moved his attention to the other corner of her mouth. "Do you want to fire me?"

"No." She wanted to make love with him. She couldn't believe how badly. It wasn't celibacy that was driving her toward him, she acknowledged in a sudden moment of lucidity. It was the overwhelming feeling that they were meant to be together. The feeling that although she'd married Ray and had tried to be a good wife to him, Joshua Farrington was the soul mate she'd been waiting for all her life. "Don't you want to ask me if I want to discourage you?"

His slow smile made her glad she wasn't depending on her legs to keep her upright. "Sweetheart, you couldn't discourage me if you tried."

"Oh?" She gasped as he deftly slid his knee between hers.

He kissed her right eyebrow. "I think I'm smitten with you."

"Smitten?"

"That's man talk for the L-word."

"Which L-word?"

He kissed her left eyebrow. "How many are there?"

"Like. Lust. Love."

He kissed the tip of her nose. "You like details, don't you?"

"I like you."

"Do you?" His wicked smile was full of promise. "I like you too. More than like you." He kissed her then, a slow, tantalizing, teasing kiss that set her on fire, nibbling first on her lower lip, then tracing her mouth with his tongue. "I want you, Liss. I can't tell you how much— Oh, hell."

Confused as he raised his head, Liss winced in surprise as the first raindrop fell on her forehead. It was followed by another. Then another bigger, fatter drop. And then, without any further warning, it started to pour, the sky opening up and dumping copious amounts of water on them.

Within seconds they were both soaked. They rapidly gathered up their picnic items and raced for the Corvette. Slamming the doors shut, they panted for breath, steaming up the windows, dripping water on the leather interior, both of them trying not to look at the other. Trying not to touch the other.

"I think we'd better get into dry clothes before we both catch pneumonia," Liss finally said, trying not to think of Josh without clothes on. She knew what would happen if she did. "Don't you?"

He glanced at her, his gaze skimming over the damp cotton stretched over her small breasts. "You're probably right." He paused, his husky voice almost like a physical touch. "Would you like to drive? Or shall I?"

Liss didn't think she *could* drive. At the moment it was all she could do to remember how to breathe.

He smiled at her mute look of appeal. "Your place?" he asked as he started the car. "Or mine?"

"Whose is closest?" Liss asked, realizing that she didn't have the faintest idea where he lived. Realizing that all she wanted to do at the moment was be alone with him, somewhere other than in the small confines of a car with a gearshift between them.

"Yours is," Josh said, shifting the Corvette into first gear. "But it's not all that close. We're halfway down the lake."

Liss dragged her gaze away from him and prayed for self-control as he pulled the car back onto the main road. Every cell in her body wanted closer contact with him. Every nerve ending tingled with awareness. All day long she'd been fighting the attraction. Fighting her conflicting emotions about him.

Their hillside picnic had somehow clarified things for her. She was no longer confused about what she wanted. She wanted him. As much, if not more, than he wanted her.

They drove a mile in heavy silence before Josh spoke again. "Do you like families?"

Not understanding the question, or why he was asking it, she turned to look at him. "I beg your pardon?"

"Sweetheart, if we don't keep talking, we're going to end up doing something else. Right here in the car, despite the fact it's still broad daylight and that this is a fairly busy road. So, do you like families?"

Liss had to take a deep breath before she could speak. "Mine or someone else's?"

He picked up her hand and squeezed it. "I'm asking if you like kids."

"I love kids," she said truthfully, and tried not to think about how they came into being. She was having a hard enough time keeping out of Josh's arms as it was. "How about you?"

"I've already got names picked out. How about gardening?"

"I'm for it." She resisted the desire to brush back a wet lock of brown hair from his forehead.

"Do you like it?" Josh sounded like he was having trouble keeping his hands to himself as well.

"I have a brown thumb."

He turned her hand over. "Looks fine to me. In fact . . ." He lifted her hand to his mouth and kissed her thumb. "I think it's irresistible."

"Are you going to flirt with me all the way home?"

"Yes and no."

"Yes and no?"

"I'm going to flirt with you. Whether or not we're going to make it home while I'm still flirting remains to be seen. Do you like the Bills?"

"I'll tolerate no criticism of the Bills," she warned, referring to her beloved, if beleaguered, football team.

"Then we're clearly meant for each other. Neither will I. Hang on. I'm taking a shortcut. And the road gets pretty bumpy."

They didn't speak again as Josh dodged water-filled potholes, taking the shortest route to her house. Once there, he wordlessly shut off the engine. Then, almost if a silent signal had been sent, they both hopped out of the car and raced to the door through the sheets of rain. Thunder boomed in the distance.

Josh watched as Liss searched her pocketbook for her keys. In spite of his teasing, and in spite of the heat coiled inside him, he had every intention of saying good-bye. Of going to his own place. Of giving her more time, and more space, to get to know him. The real him. Not the evasive, kiss-you-to-keep-you-from-asking-too-many-questions bum he'd been so far.

But, as she brought out her keys, he found himself kissing her again. Unable to control the impulse, he melded his mouth with hers, then his damp body with hers, feeling the heat of her through their wet clothes. And he knew he was lost.

"Liss . . ." It came out as half groan, half plea, full of need and wanting as he nuzzled her soft throat and felt her throbbing pulse.

He heard her take a deep breath. "Josh. I want—"

"Tell me what you want."

He could feel her confusion, and her indecision. Just as he could feel her desire welling up inside her.

He ran his hands over her bare arms and shoulders, smoothing them up and then down again, unable to keep from touching her. Unable to resist her perfumed softness.

He wanted all of her. He wanted to give her all of him.

As his hands slid down to hers he felt the cool metal of her key ring and gently removed it from her trembling fingers. Without letting her go, he turned her back to the door, pressing her against it as he slid the key into the lock and slowly turned it.

His heart slamming against his ribs, he pushed

open her door and they entered her living room, entwined in each other's arms, their lips seeking each other's hungrily, their bodies seeking closer contact.

"What about our clothes?" Liss whispered as his mouth left hers to explore the delicate swirl of her ear.

"I think we should remove them." He kissed her shoulder, smoothing his lips over the damp skin and, sending spirals of warmth roiling through Liss's veins.

She sucked in her breath as he slid the strap of her sundress off her shoulder. "I thought we were going to change them."

She could hear the smile in his voice, along with the barely suppressed passion. "You have to remove them to change them."

"You don't have a change of clothes here." She gasped as he lowered the other strap off her shoulder.

"You do." He bent over and kissed her collarbone. "Let's change yours first."

But she knew what they were going to do was make love.

"What if I don't know you well enough to undress in front of you?" she asked, feeling excited, and nervous, and so turned on she could barely stand.

Josh kissed the hollow of her throat. "You want to know about me?"

She clung to his broad shoulders for support as her knees dissolved beneath her. "Yes."

"Then let's start now." He pulled her farther into the living room and kissed her again, and again, heating her blood, stealing her breath away, melting her bones and her ability to think.

"I don't think we should be doing this here," she said when he finally lifted his mouth from hers to kiss her forehead.

"Why not?" he asked as he kissed both her cheeks.

"The curtains are open." And it was still day. Barely four o'clock in the afternoon. A decadent time to be making love. A wonderful time to be making love.

He brushed his lips against her. "So they are."

"What are you thinking?" she whispered.

"Besides how very desirable you are?" He kissed her long and hard. "I think we definitely need more privacy."

His mouth on hers again, he scooped her up into his arms and carried her into her blue-and-white bedroom. Liss sighed against his damp shoulder, boneless with wanting. The fact that they were rain-soaked made it all the more erotic. All the more exciting.

Inside the room, Josh strode past the bed to the window. He yanked closed the shades, then, with his mouth seeking hers again, let her feet slide to the floor. Her sundress soon followed the path to the cream carpet. Then his shirt, jerked over his head with one hand because he refused to let her go, even for a second.

His mouth hungrily plundering hers, they tugged off their remaining clothes, dropping them to the floor.

As soon as he'd helped divest Liss of her cotton bra and panties, Josh pulled her into his arms, holding her close to his chest. She moved against him, enjoying the warm satin of his skin, the erotic tickle of his chest hair against her bare breasts.

Letting out a low groan of suppressed desire, Josh buried his mouth in her hair, his hands sliding up and down her back, then dropping to cup her bottom. "God, you feel wonderful."

On fire with wanting, Liss smiled tremulously as she kissed the soft hair on his chest. "You feel pretty wonderful yourself."

"I want you, Liss." His voice was a husky rasp. "Like I've never wanted anything."

Liss inhaled the clean male scent that was him. "I know."

His arms tightened convulsively around her. "Do you want me? Please say yes," he added, a glimmer of his wry amusement sneaking through the rough passion in his voice. "Or I think I may go crazy."

"Yes," she said simply, irrevocably. She wanted him, more than she'd ever wanted anything. Stretching up on her tiptoes, she kissed his chin, reveling in his masculinity and the way his rougher skin abraded hers. "So, what do you plan to do about it?" she couldn't resist teasing.

"Let me show you." Even as he spoke he pushed her down onto the bed, sliding on top of her. "God, Liss." It came out as a groan as they sank down onto the bed. Liss let out a small sigh of purely feminine pleasure as he bent and kissed the soft cleft between her breasts, then moved to capture first one rosy peak in his mouth, then the other.

Filled with a piercing longing so sweet and so strong it hurt, she wove her fingers through his damp hair, loving the soft healthy feel of it.

"I thought we were going to get dry clothes on," she murmured.

Josh traced a line from her breasts down to her navel with his lips. "That comes later."

Liss sucked in her breath as he explored her navel with gentle thoroughness, swirling his tongue around the exquisitely sensitive skin. "How much later?"

"Much, much later." He moved his attention below her navel, rasping his tongue across her flat abdomen as his fingers tickled across her hipbones. "You're not in a hurry to get dressed, are you?"

"No," she managed to gasp as his fingers worked their way toward the heat between her thighs.

"Good." His voice was a low sexy purr that sent her heart straight up to her throat.

"Why is that good?" she asked as he drew small circles on her sensitized skin.

"Because I have no intention of hurrying this."

True to his word, he touched her with aching slowness, taking his time as he smoothed his hands over her body, exploring every inch of her, encouraging her to do the same to him.

So hot with desire she was certain they would burst into flame, Liss made a sound of protest when he leaned away. "Don't go."

"I wasn't going to leave you." He pushed her hair off her face. "I just had a moment of lucid thinking."

Not even close to one herself, Liss rubbed against him. "About what?"

He kissed her mouth. "About you. It occurred to me you might not be using birth control, or be otherwise prepared for a romantic encounter with the opposite sex."

"Are you calling me naive again?"

"No. I'm calling you irresistible. And maybe a little too trusting."

"And what are you?"

"Prepared, love." He kissed her on the mouth again. "And determined to protect you, whether you think you need protecting or not."

"I suppose you run around with little foil packets in your wallet all the time."

"What do you think?"

"I think you care enough about me to be careful," she whispered, feeling her desire for him swelling up inside her until she was sure she'd explode.

"That I do, sweetheart. That I do." He speared his fingers through her hair, holding her still while he covered her face with a thunderstorm of kisses.

And then, unable to wait any longer, he protected her before melding them together with a swiftness that surprised her. The soft moan that escaped her was half protest, half encouragement as their bodies joined, becoming two halves of a whole.

"Hold on, sweetheart," he whispered into her hair. "It's going to be another bumpy ride."

Wrenching a shuddery gasp of pleasure from her, he rolled her on top, kissing her throat as he moved slowly inside her at first, then with more urgency. Then, rolling back on top of her, he rested his weight on his arms and caught her hands in his. Her smooth legs entwined with his longer ones, and Liss curled her fingers around his, reveling in his strength as his movements became rougher, faster, spinning them out of control, throwing them into the maelstrom, until they both reached the pinnacle in a burst of passion as bright as the sun and burning just as hot.

Afterward Liss lay beside Josh, listening to his still rapidly beating heart, and let out a long, contented sigh. "Oh, my."

Rubbing his chin against her hair, Josh encircled her with his arms, pulling her closer. "I meant to be a

little more controlled," he confessed. "Did I hurt
you?"

Longing for him to make them one all over again,
Liss shook her head as she clasped her arms around
his waist.

"You could never hurt me," she assured him, resting her head on his chest.

As he held her and stroked her golden hair, reluctant to let her go, Josh found himself praying that she
was right, even while he knew that she was wrong.
He'd already hurt her. He'd lied to her. Now he had
to figure out what to do about it.

NINE

The next morning Josh swore heartily and at great length after he hung up the phone. He'd just had a long and not particularly pleasant conversation with his editor concerning the lateness of his usually on-time review. He simply couldn't bring himself to publish his review of the Lakeview. Not just because it wasn't particularly flattering, but because it seemed the ultimate betrayal to let it hit print without warning Liss first. He honestly didn't know what to do. For the first time that he could remember, he was balking at doing his job. He didn't want to write about Liss's restaurant the way he knew he had to in order to be honest. And certainly not before he'd confessed to her who he was.

So far he'd managed to put off the inevitable. But precisely because it was inevitable, it couldn't be avoided forever. He was going to have to get his act in gear. He had to tell Liss. Now. But he wanted to soften the blow, and he didn't know how.

He was still sitting by the phone, nursing a cooling

cup of coffee and staring blankly at the Monet print on the wall, when it rang again. He turned his head and looked at it, not moving. One ring. Two rings.

It probably wasn't his editor, he acknowledged. Bret Pierce had already said all he had to say, in his own pithy unrepeatable way. And it probably wasn't his folks, whom he'd talked to the day before. Most of his friends knew better than to call him in the middle of the day, when he was invariably writing or working on the café he hoped to open in a month or so.

Which meant it was probably a sales rep of some sort. Picking up the phone and ready to snap off the head of the person on the other end of the line, Josh sucked in his breath when he realized it was Liss. Soft, wonderfully sweet Liss. The person he most wanted to see, and most wanted to avoid talking to at the moment.

"You sound surprised," she said, sounding both cautious and nervous herself. "Have I called at a bad time?"

"You've caught me off guard." He put down his coffee cup. "I didn't think you knew my number." When he'd reluctantly left her the night before, he'd wondered when he'd see her again. And what he'd say when he did. And now here she was, innocent and unsuspecting, just when he was flagellating himself on her behalf.

"I have a friend at the phone company," she confessed. "She helped me locate you."

Josh felt as if his chest had a heavy weight on it. "That was devious of you."

He could almost see her wrinkling her tiny nose. "I thought you'd appreciate it. To tell you the truth, I was surprised to find you weren't unlisted. You being the secretive type and all." She paused, then went on a little too brightly, "Am I imposing on your privacy?"

Hearing the disquiet in her voice, Josh was quick to reassure her. "No. I'm glad you called. I've been thinking of you all morning." Lord knew, it was the truth.

"In a positive way, I hope," she said, clearly not reassured.

"When I see you," he said suggestively, even though he didn't feel the least bit seductive at the moment, "I'll show you how I've been thinking about you. I enjoyed being with you yesterday," he added truthfully. "More than you'll ever know."

"I enjoyed it too," she said. "That's why I called." She hesitated, then went on, sounding exactly like someone who was unaccustomed to asking for a date, but was determined to overcome her shyness. "Would you think I was being too forward if I invited you to go to dinner with me tonight? I'd like to try out the Dockside, to see what the competition is up to. And it's awkward eating out alone."

"Is that the only reason?" he teased. He hoped not. He hoped last night had meant as much to her as it had to him.

She hesitated again. "No. I thought we could talk. About last night."

She'd obviously been wondering, as had he, what their lovemaking would do to their relationship, how it would change. But not, he was sure, for the same reasons.

Physical involvement inevitably changed things. Josh didn't regret having taken that step with her.

Hell, he was ecstatic it had happened. It was the order of events that he regretted.

He hadn't meant for things to go this way. He'd fully intended to tell Liss who he was before they'd gotten so deeply involved. The fact that he hadn't made it that much worse.

The timing was terrible. She was going to think he'd put off his confession so she'd make love with him, knowing she probably wouldn't even talk to him after she knew the truth. She'd be justified in being suspicious. And furious. He was furious at himself.

So far, he'd handled the situation like an idiot. But maybe, just maybe, there was still time to salvage the situation.

If they went to the Dockside, he could use it for his next review, and thus put off publishing the review of the Lakeview a bit longer. And he could pass on a few more pointers for Liss to use at the Lakeview while she was still interested in taking his advice. He felt compelled to do it now, because after he told her who he was, she probably wouldn't listen to a word he said for a very long time.

Most important, though, he could use the opportunity to fess up. He wasn't above wining and dining her if it would help her be more receptive. It was worth anything, including selling his soul to the devil, if necessary, to keep from losing her.

"I'd love to have dinner with you tonight," he said.

"Shall I pick you up?" she asked.

"No. I'll drive." He made a note to send her flowers within the hour. "Why don't I pick you up at seven?"

Liss nervously looked over the menu of the nautically themed Dockside restaurant and tried not to panic.

Something was wrong. She didn't know Josh well enough to know exactly what it was, but she was certain something heavy weighed on his mind. Something he wasn't ready, or willing, to tell her about.

He'd done very little talking so far, and when he did speak it wasn't about them but about the restaurant. In fact, any mention of what had happened between them the day before was conspicuously absent from his conversation.

Being naturally insecure, Liss couldn't help wondering if he'd sent her that enormous bouquet of white roses to prime her for disappointment, and was waiting for a suitable time during dinner to tell her it was over between them. Another part of her brain, the part that was still functioning in spite of her attraction to him, wondered what "it" was.

They didn't exactly have a normal relationship. Despite the fact they'd made hot, intensely passionate love the day before, they'd never had a date until now, and then she'd done the asking.

"Try my Cajun mozzarella sticks," Josh said as she pondered whether she'd fallen into a one-night stand and hadn't even seen it coming.

Recognizing that the appetizers at the Dockside were far more interesting than anything she served, she mentally took notes as she tasted the hot, spicy deep-fried cheese sticks.

She'd already tried to find out how Josh felt about the appetizer selection, but he was being surprisingly neutral. No matter what she asked him, he nodded and made frustratingly noncommittal noises like "Mmmm," and "Ahhh."

Considering he'd been so opinionated before, especially when it came to anything involving her restaurant, his sudden neutrality struck Liss as totally suspect. It was almost as if he'd decided to let her come to her own conclusion that the appetizers she served were sadly lacking.

Not that he wasn't being his usual manipulative self, of course. He was just learning to be sneakier about it. He was a complicated man, and clearly experienced in getting what he wanted while letting a person think they were doing all the deciding.

The fact she'd figured this out probably meant, she acknowledged, that she knew him better than he'd intended her to. Liss was perfectly aware, as they ordered, that he was subtly trying to steer her to more adventurous choices, both in food and wine.

In fact, Josh had insisted on ordering a wine with their appetizers as well as one with dinner. When she questioned the need for one with dessert as well, he said that it was all part of another "wine lesson."

Not wanting to upset the applecart, at least not until they'd had a chance to discuss what had happened between them the day before, Liss went along, albeit reluctantly. It was a lot more wine than she was used to drinking. In fact, she realized, she'd drunk more wine in the past few days with him than she had in the past few years.

Dear Lord. Liss suddenly found it impossible to breathe.

Could she be dealing with an alcoholic? Was *that* what he was trying to tell her? Was that why he was looking so serious?

"How was your dinner?" he asked as she stared at her glass of port and tried not to look as worried as she felt.

"It was delicious," she said truthfully, avoiding his eyes. "They make wonderful pasta here."

And he made wonderful love. He was sensitive, and caring, and gentle, and patient, which had surprised her because she'd imagined he would be impatient to the point of roughness.

"I notice you don't have any pasta dishes on the Lakeview's menu," he said casually as she pondered her cool, smooth chocolate mousse and tried not to think about how warm and smooth his skin had felt beneath her hands.

"There's a good reason for that," she said, hoping her face wasn't showing anything of what kept tumbling through her mind. "I don't know how to make it. At least not well. I come from a meat-and-potatoes family." And Ray had never put it on the menu because he had always thought Italian food was too plebeian.

Josh, she decided, would probably think she was being plebeian for thinking that their lovemaking meant anything at all. In fact, he'd probably come to dinner with her to tell her that, and just didn't know how to get started.

"What do you think of pasta?" she asked, looking everywhere but at him.

Out of the corner of her eye, she saw him shrug. "Depends on what kind and who is cooking it."

"Did you like the rigatoni quattro formaggio?" She'd given him a taste of hers, having no idea how intimate the action would be, or how sensually aware it would make her of him.

"Mmmm."

"What about the fugilli?" He'd given her a taste of his, and she could've sworn the temperature in the room soared up ten degrees.

"Mmmm," Josh replied.

Determined to get him to commit himself, Liss made a few more remarks about how the food had been prepared and presented. Each time Josh responded with vague "Mmmms."

After the eighth one—she was counting—Liss eyed him in exasperation. "What does 'Mmmm' mean?"

"What do you think it means?"

Questions answering questions again, she noticed. "I think it means I'm supposed to be getting some sort of message here. I'm just not sure what it is. You didn't steer me toward ordering pasta because you thought it might make me sit up and take notice that my menu is somewhat lacking, did you?"

He raised an eyebrow. "Would I do something like that?"

"I don't know. Would you?"

"Why would I?"

"Because you think my menu is somewhat lacking?"

"Have I ever said your menu is lacking?"

"It's not what you say," Liss said, not for the first time. "It's what you don't say."

"What is it that you think I'm not saying?"

"For one thing, I think you're trying to get me to change my menu, but you don't want to hurt my feelings by telling me so."

He did want to spare her feelings, Josh acknowledged. He'd never done that sort of thing before he'd met her. Hadn't really cared if people perceived his remarks as criticism. Hell, giving criticism was what he did for a living.

But Liss was different. It was true, he thought she ought to change her menu, make it more interesting. But he didn't want to hurt her.

"So," she persisted, "are you?"

"I think what you offer could be a bit more interesting," he said.

"A bit more? Or a lot more?"

He hesitated. "A lot more."

"What is it that you think I should change?"

Josh considered the question. If he told the truth, she'd probably kick him under the table, then loathe him. And not necessarily in that order.

But if he didn't tell her the truth, she'd know it, and probably loathe him. Because if there was anything he'd learned about Liss Harding, it was that she despised dishonesty. Which was why he was so reluctant to tell her he'd been lying to her ever since they'd met. . . .

He'd considered a number of ways she could respond to the news and none of them boded well, for his physical health or for their relationship.

"Well?" she asked. "Are you going to tell me or not?"

Wishing he could just say what he needed to say, Josh stalled. "I don't know where to start."

"It's that bad?" Liss couldn't hide her dismay. "Tell me this. Is there anything you think I'm doing right?" When he hesitated again, she decided she might as well go for broke, because she'd never be satisfied until she knew. "Is there some reason why you won't tell me?"

"Yes," he said without hesitation.

"What is it?"

He looked her directly in the eye. "I don't want to hurt your feelings."

She refused to look away. "Why not?"

His voice was low and husky. "Because I care for you."

He *cared* for her. What the hell did *that* mean?

They stared at each other for a long moment, then Josh asked, "What are you thinking?"

Liss forced herself to smile. "I think I should add pasta to my list of possibilities."

Josh leaned back in his chair, cradling his still untasted glass of port in his long fingers. "And what's that?"

"Things I need to pursue."

"Am I on that list?"

She played with her mousse. "Do you want me to pursue you?" she asked, knowing he probably thought she already was, considering she was the one who'd asked him to dinner.

"What I want," he said, his voice even gentler than before, "is to know where I stand with you. Even now, after what happened yesterday, you're reluctant to tell me how you feel. Why?"

"Because I'm afraid," she admitted.

"Of what? Me?"

"No." Her voice was barely audible. "Of what will happen between us. Of what did happen. We made love, and I still know so little about you."

"I'd say you know quite a bit about me," he said, his voice equally soft. "Wouldn't you?"

She flushed. "You know what I mean. I don't know

who you are." Or what he was. "Or even what you like."

And she couldn't help wondering if she ever would. What if he was the type of man who would give himself physically, but never emotionally?

"I like you," he said.

She bit her lip in frustration. He liked her. He cared for her. But the phrase he'd avoided using so far was "I love you."

"The truth is," he said even while she was thinking it, "I think I love you."

Liss felt as if she were suffocating. Was he saying it because he meant it? Or because he knew it was what she wanted to hear?

"I'm not sure how you expect me to respond to that," she said, fiddling with her wineglass, afraid to believe him.

His smile was crooked as he reached out and cupped her hand. "You could reassure me I'm not barking up the wrong tree, by telling me you reciprocate."

Liss took a deep breath to relieve the tightness in her chest. "I think you know exactly how I feel about you."

"I'd still like to hear you say it."

"Why?"

"Because we're making an attempt to be honest and forthright with each other?"

She raised her eyes to his. "Since we're talking about honesty and forthrightness . . . Why do I get the feeling there's something else you want to tell me? Something important?"

"Because you're suspicious?"

She watched him refill her wineglass for the third

time while his own wine remained untouched. "Anyone would be suspicious of a man who wears expensive suits and goes around pretending he can't afford to pay for his dinner. Then twice gives the woman roses." And any woman with any sense would recognize when a man was trying to get her drunk.

"I told you. I had a sudden windfall."

"I know what you told me. I don't believe you." She pushed her glass away. "You know, I'm very tempted to get up and leave."

"Are you going to?"

"No."

"Why not?"

"Because even though you're being unbelievably annoying, I know you're right about the Lakeview. I've been trying to save the restaurant by not taking too many chances, and instead I'm slowly but surely running it into the ground by boring my customers to death."

"That's the only reason you aren't leaving?"

"No," she admitted.

"What's the other one?"

She forced herself to look him in the eye. "I think I might be in love with you."

Clearly pleased by the revelation, Josh kissed her fingers. "So why does that bother you so much?"

"Because I still don't know all that much about you."

"You know I like sports cars."

"That's not particularly reassuring. It means you're adventurous."

And she'd already been married to an adventurous man, one who took unnecessary chances. And had paid dearly for it.

"Why do I get the feeling you're making comparisons between me and Ray?"

"Because you're suspicious?" she asked mockingly.

"You talk about him, but you never really say anything about what he was like. Am I like him?"

"I'm not sure."

"Would it bother you if I was like him?"

"Yes."

"Because it would continually remind you of him?"

"In a manner of speaking."

"Is it going to be a problem?"

"I don't know yet."

"Would you like to discuss this in a more private location?"

"No." She shook her head.

"Why not?"

"Because if you take me to a more private location, I don't think we'll end up discussing anything."

"What do you think we'll end up doing?"

Liss swallowed as he brought her hand to his lips again. "Making love."

"I'll ask for the check immediately," he teased. He put his elbows on the table and leaned toward her, closing the already small gap between them. "I want to make love to you."

Even though he said it so low she could barely hear him, Liss flushed. "I know."

"I think you want to make love with me as well."

Her eyes widened in alarm as he lifted his hand. "What are you doing?"

"Signaling for the check. What did you think?"

"Why?"

"Why do you think?"

She let out an exasperated sigh. "I think you ask too many questions and give too few answers."

"Is there something you want to ask me?"

"Yes."

He signaled again for the check. "Ask away. But I warn you, you've got just until we get the check and we get outside, because the minute we're alone I'm going to kiss you senseless."

She was already without sense, Liss decided. Because she wanted him to take her outside and kiss her senseless.

"Time's almost up," he warned in a husky voice.

"So is yours," she said firmly. "Because if you don't tell me more about yourself, I'm not letting you get within ten feet of me."

Capitulating, Josh leaned back in his chair. "Okay. What's the one thing you most want to know about me?"

"Are you really not married?"

"I'm really not married. Is that what you're worried about? That I'm attached?"

"I'm worried that there's something about you I ought to know. Something important. And you're not telling."

He hesitated for so long, Liss didn't think he was going to answer. "I do have something to tell you," he finally said.

She felt a stab of anxiety. "Something important?"

"I think you might consider it important."

"What do you consider it?"

"Something you ought to know about me before our relationship goes any further."

"Oh." Even more nervous, because it wasn't what

she'd expected him to say, Liss steeled herself. "So why don't you?"

"I'd rather not do it in a public place just in case you decide to murder me. I couldn't stand it if you went to jail."

Recognizing he was trying to use humor to defuse what he clearly thought was a serious situation, Liss felt her heart begin to thump. "Then why come with me here in the first place?"

"I was hoping to wine and dine you first and I wasn't sure you'd come to my place after what happened yesterday. Would you have?"

She thought a moment before answering. "Probably not. Why did you want to wine and dine me first?"

For the first time since she'd met him, Josh looked uncomfortable. "Because I wanted you to be in a receptive mood."

"Receptive?"

"Amiable."

She thought of the bottles of wine he'd insisted on ordering. "You mean you wanted me half-drunk."

"Drunk would be nice," he said with a small, pained smile that made her all the more nervous.

"So you could have your way with me. Again."

"No, so that if you wanted to shoot me before I had a chance to explain, your aim would be off. Things progressed a little further than I'd intended yesterday."

"The way you kissed me, that can't have been too much of a surprise." Liss took a calming breath. "Am I likely to want to shoot you when you tell me whatever it is you have to tell me?"

"Very likely."

"Don't you think it might be best if you get it over with, then?"

His look was so intense and his silence so long, Liss felt as though her heart were being clutched by a large invisible hand.

"Before I start, I want to you know this," he said, all trace of humor gone as he took her hand again and gave it a small squeeze. "Nothing you could do, or say, could make me feel any more of a heel than I already do." Then, as she watched, he reached into his jacket pocket and brought out a small black book.

Liss just stared at it at first. He was going to show her his "little black book," she thought in amazement. Disappointment mingled with her initial relief as she mulled over the ramifications.

He'd clearly had plenty of women in his past, or he wouldn't need a book to record their phone numbers. All things considered, she ought to be glad he wanted to confess, although the specter of so many past affairs made her instantly think not only of all the women he could compare her with, but of health concerns as well.

The moment that thought slithered into her mind, her relief quickly dissipated. Dear Lord, was he trying to tell her that he'd contracted a dreaded disease? No, not *a* dreaded disease. *The* dreaded disease. AIDS. Even the sound of the word in her mind was like a death knell. It made her throat close, her chest hurt, and her heart physically ache.

She felt as if it was going to stop beating alto-gether. She'd never paid the least bit of attention to her heart's functioning before she'd met Josh. Ever since she had, it had raced, thumped, jumped, and did any number of ridiculous things.

And now it looked as if it was going to break.

He silently handed her the small black book. Liss took it with cold fingers. And tried not to think of how her life was likely to be irrevocably changed by its contents.

She opened it slowly, taking her time. Because time might be precious now. She didn't want to think about how they might not have much of it left after she opened the book. She didn't want to hurry it. In fact, she didn't want to open it at all.

"I think you need to see what's inside," he said, gently this time, as she continued to hesitate.

Finally Liss opened the book all the way. And when she began reading the contents, her life as she was beginning to know it came to an abrupt end.

Because it was just as bad as she'd feared. And in some ways, even worse.

TEN

Disbelief and anger mingled together until Liss couldn't breathe. She stared at the contents of the little black book in silence, sick at heart. Sick to her stomach. And thoroughly furious.

"So," she finally said, through a throat clogged with more hurt than she'd thought possible. "You're J. P. Farr. That's what you've been hiding from me."

Josh sat back in his chair when she shook off his attempt to hold her hand. "I'm afraid so."

"The one who destroys restaurants."

"The one who *critiques* restaurants," he corrected her, clearly unfazed by her bitterness.

"If you say so." Liss sat back in her own chair, afraid if she was within reach she'd bop him one. "I have to tell you, Farrington, your timing leaves a hell of a lot to be desired. I don't suppose you thought to bring it up before we got a little more than just professionally involved."

"I know how this looks. Believe me, I intended to tell you before we made love—"

"You didn't try very damned hard." Liss tried to

pull air into her constricted chest. "I think we both know there wouldn't have been a chance in hell we'd have made love if you'd told me," she added, daring him to deny it.

He didn't. He looked at her a long time before speaking, and when he did speak, Liss knew he was fighting the urge to take her into his arms.

"I didn't expect you to believe me. In your place, I probably wouldn't either. I knew you'd feel like this. It's why I've been beating my brains out all day trying to figure out how to convince you I'm not that conniving." Liss snorted in disbelief. "Would you like to go outside where we can discuss this in private?"

Just from the way he said it, Liss knew he was waiting for some sort of explosion. "No," she said emphatically.

His gaze took in her tight-lipped mouth. "Why not?"

"Because if we leave here and go somewhere more private, I'm likely to murder you, that's why not."

He nodded, unsurprised by her vehemence. "You have every right to be angry."

"I'm not angry," Liss said. She was sick at heart. And furious. Beyond furious. She was practically beyond coherent thought.

Ever since she'd met him, she'd known there was more to him than met the eye. More than he was telling. But for some reason it had never, ever occurred to her that he was the enemy.

But the worst part wasn't that he'd pulled a fast one on her. The worst part was that she'd liked him. Had more than liked him. Was falling head over heels in love with him. And he'd known it. He'd let it happen. He hadn't done a thing to stop it, even though, by his own admission, he knew exactly how she'd feel when she found out the truth.

"I assume you were reviewing the Lakeview the night you claimed you couldn't pay for your dinner?" she asked when she could finally speak.

He hesitated. "Yes."

"And I suppose the bit about your being broke and unable to pay was some sort of little game you play when you're bored with your food." She was losing her composure, Liss realized, and she didn't give a damn.

"Pretending I couldn't pay was part of my reviewing process," he said, accepting her wrath without making any excuses for himself. "I don't judge just the food, I judge an establishment in its entirety."

She looked down at the small book in her hand. "Are your notes from that night in here?"

"Yes. On page forty-four."

Handling it with undisguised distaste, Liss quickly paged through the book. Her stomach clenched into a knot as she noticed the notations under the heading *Firestone*. She stopped flicking through the pages when she came to the one headed *Lakeview*.

She looked up at Josh, who was watching her closely. "Would you mind if I read them?" she asked.

"Could I stop you?"

"No." Liss was amazed at how calm she sounded when all she wanted to do was throttle him. "I just wanted to know if you objected to me seeing them before your review hits print. You *are* going to put your review in the paper, I trust?"

"It's been scheduled for the day after tomorrow."

Which was why he'd come out with her tonight, Liss realized. Part of her recognized that he was trying to let her know who he was and what he was going to say before the review was printed, to save her from the probable shock. The rest of her recognized that she was so mad at him at the moment, she didn't care what his motivation was.

Josh watched with unnatural stillness as she began reading his notes. They were neat and tidy despite the fact that he probably had to make them on the sly, Liss noted caustically. The notes were pretty caustic themselves.

"You didn't like the stuffed mushrooms?" she asked, trying not to sound as if she cared. In fact, the stuffed mushrooms were not only a sentimental issue for her—the recipe was her grandmother's—she also considered them one of the Lakeview's pluses.

"The mushrooms were very nice," he answered so carefully, she knew he wasn't saying something, again.

"But?" she prodded tersely, not caring a hoot or a holler that he'd apparently taken her "Say something nice, then lower the boom" lesson to heart.

"But you don't do enough with them."

"What would you suggest?" she sniped. "Mushrooms flambé?"

"Are you asking me for suggestions?"

"I'm asking you for a reason why I shouldn't dump my glass of wine over your head then bean you with the bottle."

He smiled slightly, but not, she noticed, without effort. "For one thing, it's too good a vintage to waste. For another, even if you're justifiably mad, you don't really want to hurt me."

"Don't be too sure of that," she muttered into her glass of the vintage she was still considering lofting at him. After a moment of anything but comfortable silence, she gave in to an overwhelming sense of curiosity and asked in a voice laced with sarcasm, "What, specifically, don't you like about my stuffed mush-rooms?"

Josh closed his mouth, looking like he wasn't going to answer. Then, almost as if recognizing that she needed to vent her anger at him in order to forgive him, he said, "They're too ordinary."

Ordinary? She gave him a withering glare. "What the devil does *that* mean?"

"It means you ought to try using your imagination more."

"I'm using my imagination right now," she informed him. And it didn't bode well for his physical well-being.

He seemed unsurprised by her remark. "I don't doubt it. Is my good health in danger?"

"You'd better believe it. The only reason you're still in one piece is because I know the owner of this restaurant. I don't want to lose him any business by creating a scene. Otherwise, you'd be dead meat."

"That's what I like most about you," Josh said. "You're such a thoughtful woman."

"I'm an outraged woman," she snapped back. "And a wronged one."

He reached over and retrieved the black notebook from her hand before she could shred it in retaliation. "It's not that I don't think I deserve your wrath, but I'd like to know something."

"Which is?"

"What's making you so angry? My true identity? Or the fact that you like me?"

"I liked who you *were*," she retorted. "Or who I thought you were. Not what you are."

He slid the book into his jacket pocket. "And what am I?"

"A cheat and a liar. The kind of man who makes a living off other people's talents. You know the saying— 'Those that can, do. Those that can't, criticize.' "

He shook his head. "I don't buy that. What really bothers you about me being a critic?"

"You honestly don't know?" Liss looked at him in open scorn. "You don't care who you hurt. You drop in and do a hit-and-run, staying just long enough to see what's wrong with a restaurant, but never long enough to see the reason why something may not live up to your sky-high expectations. Anyone can have a bad night. Help that doesn't show up. Temperamental chefs having snit fits. Or a case of the flu. Food that doesn't get delivered. Not that you care. You're inhuman, Farr. And what's worse," she added, knowing she was hurting him and not caring, "you don't even seem to know it."

He didn't speak at first. When he did, his voice was rough with emotion. "So, what can I do to make it up to you?"

"I can't think of anything. Other than you disappearing."

He studied her face, slowly, thoroughly, almost as if he wasn't sure when he'd get the chance to again. "Then it's over between us."

Liss forced herself to say the words she knew would end their relationship. "You could say that."

"Are you saying that?"

For one terrible moment she thought she was going to lose it and burst into tears of frustration. And outrage.

He didn't truly think things could ever be the same

between them, did he? She didn't know what made her madder. Him being who he was, or her liking him, even loving him, and not guessing that the man beneath the charming, likable facade was a rat of the first order. A rat who made a career out of putting other people down.

Could she ever forget who he was and what he did for a living? Not in a million years.

"What I'm saying," Liss said, slowly and carefully, "is that I never want to see you again. Ever."

And then, with knees that shook so badly she doubted she could make it to the door without assistance, she got up. Holding on to the back of her chair, she paused long enough to look down at him. "Oh, and by the way. You're fired." And then she walked out of the restaurant, and out of his life.

In true Farr fashion, Josh refused to stay out of her life. At least, for very long.

"You're not going to believe this," Rob said to her two nights later. He'd already heard an abbreviated, but definitely not unemotional, version of what had happened at the Dockside the night before last. He'd clearly been trying not to say "I told you so" ever since.

"Oh, I don't know," Liss said, slapping together a chocolate torte with such vehemence that Rob winced. "I can believe almost anything." She could even believe she'd fallen in love with a man who was a dishonest, lying, cheating skunk. What she couldn't believe was how much she missed him. "What are you doing?" she demanded as Rob carefully removed the knife from her hand.

He smiled benignly. "Trying to prevent a murder."

"Who am I likely to murder?"

"Come look out into the dining room, and you tell me."

Blowing out a stream of air in exasperation, Liss walked to the swinging door and looked out into the dining room.

Rob was right. She couldn't believe it. Scowling at the vision of Josh Farrington seated at a table in the rear, she turned and gave Rob a homicidal glare.

"Why the devil did you let him in?" she railed at him.

"I tried to stop him," Rob said. "He pointed out to me that if I attempted to get him to leave, he'd not only create a scene that would make the front page of the local newspaper—where he works and has connections, by the way—he also threatened to call in the American Civil Liberties Union."

"On what grounds?"

"For refusing him service."

"I can serve, or not serve, anyone I please," Liss snapped, furious at Josh. And furious at herself. Just seeing him again in the dark suit and tie, with his neatly trimmed hair and innate sensuality and self-assurance, was making her heart pound, her head swim.

"Not without posting a notice to that effect," Rob said.

Liss clenched her teeth together until it hurt. "Who told you that?"

"Farr. Who else? He offered to have his lawyer call and explain it to you, but I thought that would just make you madder."

"I don't think it's possible for me to be madder." Liss untied her apron and stomped out to the dining room, marching directly to his table. "What do you think you're doing?" she whispered at him, making no attempt to hide the fact that she'd just as soon behead him as talk to him.

Looking up from the menu in his hands, Josh smiled at her. "I'm planning on having dinner."

"Not in my restaurant you're not. I can refuse service to someone if I want to."

He shook his head. "*Au contraire*. Not without having a good reason, you can't, as I pointed out to your brother-in-law. He doesn't like me much, does he?"

"No one here likes you at all. And I can refuse service to someone I think is obnoxious."

"I haven't even begun to get obnoxious yet," Josh assured her.

She scowled at him. "What does that mean?"

"It means I have something to say to you. I'd prefer it if you sat down so we can talk like two civilized human beings, but if you want to stand up so you can stomp your foot while you have a temper tantrum, that's fine by me."

"I'm not having a temper tantrum," Liss told him, still standing. "And I'm not interested in hearing your apologies."

"That's good. Because I didn't come to apologize."

She blinked in surprise. "You didn't?"

"No."

"What did you come for, then?"

"Sit down and I'll tell you."

Liss eyed him as she sat down across from him. He didn't look as cocksure as usual, she noticed as he sipped from his water glass. "Well?" she asked.

He rested his hands on the table, lacing his fingers

together. "I presume you noticed that my review of the Lakeview wasn't in tonight's paper?"

She had noticed. Instead, he'd done a review on the Dockside, the restaurant they'd gone to the night all hell had broken loose. Which showed he wasn't just a fast talker, she thought caustically, he was a fast writer as well. And her being furious at him obviously hadn't given him even a slight case of writer's block.

It probably hadn't caused him to lose a wink of sleep, either, even though his confession had given her a walloping case of insomnia.

She folded her arms across her chest. "So?"

"So, I thought you should know that I pulled it."

"Your tossing out the review doesn't make me any less mad at you."

"I didn't think it would. And I didn't toss it. I pulled it for the time being."

"Why?"

"Because I'm planning on expanding it."

Expanding it? What did that mean? Liss hadn't a clue. So she asked.

Josh picked up the menu and perused it, so she couldn't see his face. "Your comment that I do hit-and-runs smarted. I've decided to give the Lakeview another chance. Admittedly, it's going to be hard to do a neutral review, considering what's happened, but I think I can handle it."

"What you can do," Liss said, "is go to hell. I'm not giving you another chance to ruin my restaurant."

"Maybe you ought to see the original before you make a final decision. I'd hate to have to put this review in, but if I have to, I will." Josh slid a neatly typed page in front of her. "My editor expects a review of the

Lakeview. It can be this one, or a revised one. He doesn't care. I thought you might, however."

Looking at it like it was a poisonous snake, Liss finally picked up the sheet of paper and skimmed it. Appalled by the scathing review, she could barely read by the time she got to the end. She was literally seeing red.

"What do you want?" she demanded. "A bribe to do a more favorable review?" At this point, she wouldn't put anything past him.

He leaned back and studied her. "That's an interesting suggestion. What are you offering?"

His hooded look told her the only thing he really wanted was her. Unfortunately, even as mad at him as she was, she still wanted him, as well. Every cell in her body tingled with awareness at his presence.

Swallowing dryly, Liss ignored both the question and the hot burning desire in his eyes. "What do you want?" she repeated.

"I told you. I want to do a neutral, honest, in-depth review of the Lakeview."

He probably also had a bridge he wanted to sell her.

Not sure if she was hearing what she thought she was hearing, Liss frowned and tried to keep the resentment out of her voice. "What does that mean, exactly?"

His smile did nothing to reassure her. "It means I don't do hit-and-runs. I try to give fair reviews. Sometimes I catch people at their worst moments. Sometimes people have nothing but worst moments. It's not always easy to figure out which. It's come to my attention that I need more time to do a balanced review of the Lakeview and I'm asking for your cooperation."

"I have no intention of giving you a second chance to torpedo my restaurant," she said, suspecting that what he really wanted was another chance to seduce her. Or get even.

He shrugged. "I can do it with or without your cooperation. Or I can publish the review as it's written. It's up to you."

Liss clamped her mouth shut before she said something she'd live to regret.

"You might try being more amenable," he went on. "All things considered, I can do you a lot of harm, or a lot of good."

Liss heard the underlying threat, knew what it would take to save her restaurant from sure disaster, and could barely speak she was so mad. "Are you trying to blackmail me?"

His eyebrows rose slightly. "I'm trying to reason with you. I don't know why you're having so much trouble receiving criticism, since you seem to have no qualms about dishing it out yourself."

It was the truth. Liss had plenty of criticism about his profession in general, and his mode of working in particular. She especially hated the way he sneaked in, catching people on a bad night.

Clearly, what the man needed was to be more understanding.

Actually, what he needed, Liss decided, warming to the idea that had just sprouted in her mind, was to put the shoe on the other foot and learn a lesson in humility. Not to mention why it wasn't wise to try to blackmail stubborn independent women.

"I have a proposition for you," she said.

He leaned back in his chair, his smile full of male satisfaction. "I didn't expect this to be so easy. You don't look like the propositioning type. Where shall we meet and when?"

"I meant a professional proposition," she clarified.

"I was afraid you'd say something like that. What is it?"

"You don't think I'm doing a very good job running the Lakeview, do you?"

Josh took his time answering. "Truthfully? No." It was a little blunter than he'd intended, but he had a feeling this was no time for wishy-washy answers.

"You think there are all sorts of things I could do better, don't you? In fact, you think just about anyone could do a better job. You, for instance."

"I couldn't do too much worse," he said, not sure what she was leading up to, but happy that she was at least talking to him.

She smiled tightly. "So, do it."

"Do what?"

"Do a better job of running a restaurant than I have."

"Do you have any particular restaurant in mind?"

"The Lakeview, of course."

"And then what?"

"After a week I get to write a review."

The little munchkin was serious. Josh couldn't believe what he was hearing.

"Aren't you afraid I'll run it into the ground, me being so recalcitrant and all?"

She shrugged. "I have nothing to lose. Even if you write a revised review, things being what they are, the restaurant will be as good as finished. If you run the Lakeview badly, at least I can blame you when it fails."

Josh studied her. He knew he should say no. She knew, as well as he did, that it took more than a week to make or break a restaurant. Even if he knew a thousand ways to improve the Lakeview—and he did—it might not be enough to save it. He certainly couldn't do it without her cooperation.

On the other hand, the only way to salvage his relationship with Liss was to prove to her he wasn't the monster she'd made him out to be. To prove to her how sorry he was. And he couldn't do that if she wouldn't let him near her. Which was why he'd come tonight.

He still couldn't believe he'd actually hinted at blackmail, but desperate situations called for desperate measures. Letting her think she could bribe him, sexually or otherwise, into a more favorable review was reprehensible, but he didn't think she'd take him seriously. He figured she knew him well enough by now to know better. But the fact she'd at least wondered if he meant it showed how much his being J. P. Farr affected her judgment, particularly of him.

"What would you be doing while I was trying to improve the Lakeview?" he asked.

She lifted her shoulders. "I was thinking I might take a vacation. I haven't had one for almost three years."

"Think again."

She blinked at him, clearly taken back by his terseness. "I beg your pardon?"

"If I'm going to try to make this place turn a profit, I expect you to be here, paying attention, taking copious notes, and learning how to take over when I'm done. And I'll need at least a month."

"God created the world in a lot less time," Liss said, looking like she knew exactly why he wanted her around, and it wasn't to take notes.

"God wasn't dealing with a pigheaded woman."

"I'll give you two weeks," she said in begrudging compromise.

"Three weeks. And that's my last offer."

She scowled at him. "Or else what?"

He smiled at her. "Or else I reconsider redoing my review." Knowing she'd take exception to it, he chucked her lightly under the chin as he rose from the table.

Her scowl darkened. "Where are you going?"

"Home, of course. I'll be back at seven tomorrow." He smiled at her consternation. "Be prepared to meet me with an open mind."

"Seven is right in the middle of the dinner rush. More likely you'll be met with an armload of dinner plates."

"Seven A.M.," he clarified. "Not seven P.M."

"I sleep in until eight."

"You *used* to sleep in until eight. The restaurant is under new management. And so are you."

"I don't need managing!"

"No." His voice was as silky as his smile was dangerous. "You need a good kissing. Possibly a good shaking. Unfortunately, you and I are going to be too busy the next couple of weeks to explore those subjects. So pull your claws in and get a good night's rest. You're going to need it."

ELEVEN

What she needed was to have her head examined, Liss decided as she waited impatiently for Josh to show up the next morning. She knew perfectly well what was going to happen if the two of them spent very much time together. And so, she suspected, did he. Which was probably why he'd blackmailed her into a deal in the first place.

Angry or not, she was going to have trouble dealing with her feelings for him. Especially if he didn't cooperate and keep his distance. Unsure how she should handle him, Liss waited with trepidation for him to arrive. When he finally appeared, it was seven thirty-five.

"You're late," she said as he breezed in the front door.

Not at all bothered by her foul mood, he waved a finger at her and scolded, "Never criticize the manager. It's bad karma."

Liss could practically feel the steam coming out of her ears. Tugging her hot-pink T-shirt down over her jeans, she put her hands on her hips. "You are *not* the manager," she said, putting as much ice into her voice as there was heat in her face. "I am. I'm also the owner. Which means you do what I say."

"Not for the next three weeks I don't." He poured himself a cup of coffee from the pot she had prepared while she waited for him, then perched on a table and smiled at her. "You aren't reneging on our deal, are you?"

Liss was furious at him. And furious at herself. Mostly she was furious because even though she knew who he was, and had told herself repeatedly that she loathed him, she knew deep down that she cared for him.

Even worse, she cared for his opinion. About her, and what she did, and how she did it, especially when it came to the restaurant.

He knew it too. Which only served to make her more furious.

"I'll tell you what," he said. "Since you obviously wish we'd never met, let alone made love, let's try to forget everything that's gone before and start over." Without waiting for her reply, he extended his hand. "Hi. I'm Josh Farrington. Among other things, I'm a restaurant critic. I publish reviews under the name of J. P. Farr, and I've been known to make a donkey's behind of myself. And you are . . . ?"

"Liss Harding, restaurateur," Liss responded, putting her hands behind her back. "And not as gullible as I used to be."

He smiled again. "Pleased to meet you."

Liss refused to smile back. He was obviously counting on her attraction to him to make her see that he really wasn't the guy in the black hat. In fact, he seemed determined to prove to her that his was pristine white.

As she sat, giving him a wary look, he handed her a chocolate doughnut. "What's this?" she asked, reluctantly taking it.

"I call it breakfast." He chewed on his glazed doughnut. "You didn't eat before you came, did you?"

"No."

"That's what I thought." He took another sip of coffee. "You know, it wouldn't hurt my feelings if you said thank you."

Feeling like an ungracious lout, Liss conceded defeat. "Thank you." She finished the doughnut, then said, "It wouldn't hurt my feelings if you apologized for being half an hour late."

He acknowledged the rebuke with a wry smile. "I got stuck behind a tractor going five miles an hour. I'm sorry I was late." He reached into the white bakery bag. "How about another doughnut?"

Surprisingly hungry, considering she'd passed on breakfast for years until he'd shown up, Liss accepted the chocolate-iced doughnut. "Thank you."

"You're welcome."

More comfortable with him than she knew she should be, considering she was trying to forget that they knew each other in the biblical sense, Liss sighed. "We always seem to be eating. Don't you ever think of anything but food?"

He licked a sticky finger. "Sure I do. I think about you all the time. How sweet and generous you are." His gaze dropped to her slim hips. "How sexy you are in jeans . . ."

She snorted. "Flattery is going to get you nowhere."

"Now, Melissa," he chided, clearly trying to humor her. "Don't you know that forgiveness is the mark of greatness?"

"On the contrary. Forgiveness is usually the result of forgetfulness. And my name isn't Melissa."

Josh finished his doughnut and refilled both their coffee cups. "I assumed that's what Liss was short for. I don't suppose, you being ticked off at me and all, you'd care to tell me your true name?"

Liss hesitated. Then, seeing no reason why he shouldn't know, she said, "Liss is short for Mélisande."

"An unusual name for an unusual woman. Where does it come from?"

"My mom got it from a book. She's a romantic."

"Are you?"

Liss sipped her coffee. "Am I what?"

"A romantic?"

She refused to respond to the warmth in his eyes. "I used to be."

"Don't."

Hearing the gentle scolding, reminded of the intimacy they'd shared, Liss fought down the heat coiling inside her. "Don't what?"

"Don't make me feel any worse than I already do. I'm trying to redeem myself. You might not feel like helping me, but at least don't fight me."

"I can't help it," she said truthfully. "Every time I think about what you did I get mad all over again."

"I thought you might feel that way, so I brought you something." He extracted a tiny tissue-wrapped object from his shirt pocket and handed it to her.

"What is it?"

"Open it and find out."

She did, and looked at the small, exquisite fox miniature in silence. Damn the man. How could she stay mad at him when he insisted on being so nice? She looked up at him. "Why?"

"I thought you needed an addition to your collection."

"The *real* reason," she said, turning the detailed figurine over in her fingers.

"I wanted you to have something to remind you of me."

"In that case"—she gave him a sweet smile—"wouldn't a skunk have been more appropriate?"

"Tsk. Your temper is showing again. I'll have you know the skunk is a much maligned animal."

"If you say so."

"I'll tell you what I have to say." He leaned forward and whispered in her ear.

Shocked in spite of herself, Liss quickly leaned away. "What are you doing?"

He smiled. "Whispering sweet somethings."

She shook her head at him. Sweet, nothing. His murmured remarks had been suggestive and sexy and anything but sweet.

He wiped his fingers on a napkin and stood up. "Ready to go to work?"

Surprised by his sudden briskness, Liss rose more slowly. "What are we going to do?"

"I thought we could talk about making some changes."

Her inner alarm system went on full alert. "What kinds of changes?"

"Well, for one thing, the all-green color scheme of the dining room is too stodgy for some of the changes

I had in mind. I thought we might walk through the restaurant with new eyes."

"What's wrong with the ones I have?" she asked, fighting to hold on to her anger at him. She had to agree with him that the green decor was all wrong. "Wrong color for you?"

"The color of your eyes is just fine," Josh said, unperturbed by her sarcasm. "They just seem to be shortsighted. Not to mention a little narrow in focus."

"They can see through you just fine," she assured him. She stopped, momentarily shocked into silence as he backed her up against the wall. He planted a hand on either side of her, preventing her escape.

"Are you going to be this bitchy the whole time I'm here?" he asked while she looked at him in wide-eyed alarm.

"I'm not being bitchy. You're being overly critical. Again."

Josh studied her flushed face. "Does this mean you don't want to change anything?" He was standing so close, she could feel the heat from his body radiating toward her.

"It means I can't afford to redecorate," she said, inhaling the masculine tang of his sandlewood after-shave. "I'm not made out of money."

"Nor sugar and spice either, from what I can tell."

She tried not to focus on the small sexy cleft in his cleanly shaven chin. "What do you want me to do? Simper and say 'yes, sir' every time you tell me what's wrong with the Lakeview?"

"No. I expect you to listen with an open mind and consider that I might be right." When she wouldn't look at him, he took her chin in his fingers, forcing her eyes to meet his. "Or would that make it too hard for you to keep on hating me?"

The trouble was, she didn't hate him. Oh, she was mad at him. Mostly because he'd known how she'd feel about who he was and had put off telling her. He'd obviously hoped that by making love to her, he'd entice her into caring for him too much for it to matter.

She was quickly discovering that being annoyed at someone was wholly different from actually hating him. You could be furious at someone and still be totally enamored with him.

She looked at him for a minute, then said hesitantly, "I don't hate you. I hate what you do."

He brushed her hair off her cheeks, his movements both gentle and erotic. "And just what is that?"

Refusing to think about the soothing ministrations of his strong fingers, Liss plunged on, "You criticize everything and everyone without considering what effect your words will have."

"I'm considering the effect of my words on you now," he said in a husky voice that made her feel weak in the knees.

"Which ones?" she asked, raising a questioning eyebrow. "The ones in your review when you pointed out that the Lakeview has all the ambience of a wet basement?"

Josh stroked her nape. "The ones when I say I love you. I do, you know. I think I loved you the second I set eyes on you."

"You're just saying that so I'll cooperate with your scheme to take over the Lakeview."

He explored the throbbing pulse in the hollow of her throat. "I'm saying it because it's true. I love you,

Liss. I love the fight in you. I especially love the way you won't give up. Even when you're wrong."

"What am I wrong about now?" she asked, refusing to acknowledge the rest of his proclamation.

"For one thing, I have no desire to take over the Lakeview. For another thing, you're wrong about me. I don't criticize everything and everyone. I've done some very complimentary reviews."

"Calling my grandmother's stuffed mushrooms 'pedestrian' was not complimentary. It was snide."

He eyed her with interest. "You're not going to take everything I say about the Lakeview personally, are you?"

"It's my restaurant. How can I not take it personally?"

"Did you decorate it?"

She hesitated before admitting, "No. Ray did."

"Did Ray decide to put Plexiglas on the tables and to use paper napkins?"

"No." Flushing under his look, she added, "I had to do something. I couldn't afford to send a hundred tablecloths and napkins to the laundry every day. What does that look mean?"

"It means I think maybe you should give up the battle."

"You mean, give up the Lakeview?" She couldn't disguise her dismay. "No way."

"Stop looking at me like that. All I'm saying is that maybe you should consider switching from elegant to something more casual. Maybe go country French. Or promote more of a bistro atmosphere. Have some fun with it. You know," he chided, tugging on her earlobe, "redecorating doesn't have to be expensive. Not if you use your imagination. Good used pieces can be gotten for a song."

"I can't sing," she said, determined not to respond to his touch. "And I don't know anything about decorating." She did, however, have quite an imagination, and it was hyperactive at the moment with thoughts of her and Josh, alone. In bed.

"Then it's a good thing you have me to rely on, isn't it? Because, as it happens, I do. I minored in design in college. All we have to do," he decreed, "is throw out everything and gut the place."

She gave him a look that would have discouraged a lesser man. "You might as well save your breath. I can't afford the time and money it would take to redo the whole place. Even if I wanted to, which I don't."

"You can't afford not to change. There's more to running a restaurant than just providing good food, you know."

"I got the feeling you didn't think the food was particularly good either," she said, still smarting from his derogatory remark about her stuffed mushrooms.

"I didn't say it wasn't good." He ran his thumb over her collarbone. "It's just not overly interesting. Except for the desserts. Those are exceptional."

"I suppose you're going to want to change the menu next," she said, melting under his touch despite her best efforts. "Then hire all new help to serve it."

"First things first. We've got other business to attend to before we start discussing changing the menu."

"Like what?"

"Like this."

He kissed her. Pressed against the wall, Liss let out a gasp of protest as he lowered his head and captured her lips in an openmouthed kiss that sent bolts of electricity straight down to her toes. Then, gathering her into his arms, he sampled her mouth at leisure, tracing her lips with his tongue, seeking entrance.

"Open your mouth for me," he said in a low voice that threatened Liss's resolve to keep her body upright and her mouth shut.

She adamantly shook her head.

"Why not? You're not afraid of me, are you?"

"Of course not . . ." Too late, she realized what he was up to.

Taking advantage of the opportunity, he urged her lips apart and explored the moist recesses of her mouth, slowly, thoroughly. Lost in sensation, Liss needed a full minute before she finally came to her senses and planted her hands on his chest.

With obvious reluctance, Josh released her.

Totally confused by her desire for him, Liss took a deep breath. "How dare you?" She knew it sounded like something out of B movie, but she was unable to come up with anything more literate.

"I dare a lot more than that." He tweaked her earlobe. "You know, that's your problem. You're afraid to take chances."

"*You* are my problem," she corrected him, slapping his hand away.

And why she'd challenged him to do a better job running the Lakeview, she didn't know. It hadn't been because she'd wanted to see him again. Had it?

He caught her hand and pressed it to his chest. "You haven't redecorated, not just because you don't have the money," he went on as if she hadn't spoken, "but because you're afraid of doing something wrong. Of making mistakes. Which is a major mistake."

"I am not afraid to redecorate. If I had the money I'd do it in a second." She was startled when he suddenly released her and pulled his checkbook and a pen from the back pocket of his jeans. "What are you doing?"

"Writing out a check," he said.

"Why are you writing out a check?"

"You said you'd redecorate if you had the money." He signed his name with a flourish and ripped the check out of the checkbook. "So, here's the money. I challenge you to make this restaurant look like someplace I'd like to bring my mother." He attempted to hand Liss the check.

She stared at it, not taking it. "People like you don't have mothers. You're spawned. Like the devil."

"Trust me. I have a mother. And I have every intention of bringing her here, so you'd better take the money. Because if you think I'm outspoken and opinionated, you haven't seen anything yet."

Ignoring her protests, he thrust the check into her hand and closed her fingers tightly around it. And then, to her annoyance, he walked away from her even while she was still protesting.

He wasn't going to take no for an answer, Liss concluded four frustrating hours, and about a thousand "no ways," later.

"I don't want this," she said for the umpteenth time as he sat at a table in the rear of dining room and continued jotting down notes—which he wouldn't let her see—on a notepad.

"Yes, you do. You just don't want anything from

me. Which is too bad, considering I'm the only one likely to give it to you."

He was the only one likely to give her an ulcer as well. And she told him so. "You never said anything about changing the restaurant when I challenged you to try running it."

"If I had, you never would've let me get near you or the Lakeview, you being peeved at me and all." He smiled at her. "A man's gotta do what a man's gotta do."

"You can't buy my affection, if that's what you had in mind."

That got to him. Apparently realizing for the first time how his offer of cold, hard cash looked to Liss, he gave her a long, thoughtful look before he spoke.

"Is that what you think I'm trying to do? Buy you?"

"I don't know what you're trying to do," she admitted, knowing instinctively from his flat tone of voice that she'd hurt him. "But I don't need a knight with a large wallet to rescue me, if that's what you're thinking. I can take care of myself. And my restaurant."

"I didn't think you couldn't. I was trying to help."

"Maybe I don't want your help."

"Or maybe you do, but you don't want this arrangement to smack of anything even remotely related to me trying to buy your love and loyalty." He leaned back and studied her as he tapped his pen on his knee. "Would you accept the money if it was a loan and not a gift? And you were certain there were no strings attached?"

She hesitated, then said, "Probably."

Clearly pleased that she wasn't going to insist on

being totally unreasonable, Josh thought a moment. "What if we called it a remodeling loan? You can pay me back just as soon as business picks up."

"It doesn't matter what you call it, I still don't have the faintest idea where to start."

"At the risk of offending your sense of assertiveness, why don't you start at the top—literally—and work your way down? It's always been my favorite modus operandi."

She narrowed her eyes in suspicion. "What does that mean?"

"It means new lights would be nice. The green shades on these make everyone look ill." He handed her a brochure of lighting fixtures. "Which would you like?"

She looked them over without enthusiasm. "What if I said none?"

"Then I kiss you until you come to your senses," Josh said, sounding infinitely reasonable.

He would too.

Knowing that his kisses made her lose her common sense, not to mention her ability to think, Liss focused her attention on the light fixtures so she wouldn't be tempted to look at his mouth. "I sort of like this one," she said, indicating her choice.

"It's my pick as well." He gave her a maddening smile. "You see? We have all sorts of things in common."

"If you say so."

"I do say so. When we pick out new drapes and furniture, you'll see that I'm right."

Liss came to full attention. "What new drapes and furniture?" She'd honestly thought he'd been joking about tossing out the furnishings and gutting the place.

"The new drapes and furniture that are going to give the Lakeview its fresh new look and some of the style its owner has, but is afraid to demonstrate, of course. Which do you like better? Dark blue and cream? Or rose and cream?"

"How about green?" she said, deadpan.

He shook his head. "Not one of the choices."

"Blue then. Dark blue." She frowned. "What *are* you smiling at?"

He looked totally innocent. "Nothing. I think you could use a few pictures on the wall, as well. There are a number of struggling local artists who could use the exposure. Some plants would be nice. A large mirror in the foyer. Vases of fresh flowers on every table. No more Plexiglas. The tables are oak. With a more casual look, you can do without tablecloths entirely, if you like." He paused while she tried to absorb everything. "I'd say the Victorian style of the building would show off antiques quite well, wouldn't you?"

Not sure what she thought about antiques, Liss balked. "I don't know anything about antiques."

"Not to worry. I'll give you lessons tomorrow. We'll hit a couple of shops. . . ." He stopped at her look. "Problem?"

"I can't go furniture hunting tomorrow. I have a restaurant to run, remember?"

"I'm running it for the next three weeks. Remember? And, as manager, I've decided we'll close temporarily for renovations."

"You've *what*?"

Ignoring her look of astonishment, Josh repeated, "I've decided we'll close temporarily for renovations."

"My help will leave me. Or is that part of the plan? To run me out of business?"

"Your help won't leave you. They're on paid vacation for a week."

"Who's paying them?"

Josh smiled. "I am, of course. It's included in the loan."

"You can't do this," she said, shaking her head.

"I *am* doing it. You gave me control of the restaurant for three weeks. Remember?"

"I did not give you control. You *took* control. There's a big difference."

To her consternation, he moved in on her again. "You know," he said in a smoky voice that made her toes curl, "if I didn't know better, I'd think you're objecting to everything I say on principle, just to be contrary."

Liss swallowed hard as she realized he'd backed her, literally, into a corner. "Why would I do that?"

"To keep me at a distance?"

She tried not to purr as he stroked her throat. "It doesn't seem to be working very well."

"That's because I'm persistent."

"You mean pigheaded," she said, exquisitely aware of the faint roughness of his fingertips, the smooth texture of his dark blue shirt. "And determined to get your own way."

"That too."

She reached up and stilled his hand as he started to draw a line down between her breasts. "What exactly is getting renovated? Or do I get any say at all in the matter?"

"I meant to discuss that with you before you distracted me."

"I did not distract you. You attacked me." In fact, every time she disagreed with him, he had the dismaying habit of making a pass at her.

"We could go over the situation again," he suggested, moving even closer to her, "and clarify that."

"Touch me again," she warned, "and I won't be responsible for what happens."

"That sounds promising."

She shot him a quelling look. "What's getting renovated?"

"I thought larger windows and a trellised patio overlooking the lake would be nice."

"Who's going to do the work?" she asked, resigned to seeing more changes, just as soon as he thought he could talk her into them.

"I've hired some students from the vocational school in Flint. They'll do it for half of what a contractor would."

Surprised by the sensible suggestion, Liss considered him. "How much experience do they have?"

"You're asking an awful lot of questions for someone who says she doesn't know anything about renovating."

"I can't help myself. When someone threatens to gut my restaurant, my sense of curiosity gets activated. You didn't answer the question," she added, remembering his annoying habit of asking questions to keep from answering any.

"What question is that?"

"How much carpentry experience do they have?"

"None to my knowledge."

"None!"

"They've been doing mostly auto mechanics."

"So have them renovate your car, not my restaurant!"

"My car doesn't need renovating. The Lakeview does. Someone has to give them their first job," he said in explanation, "or they'll never get any experience."

That stopped her. Recognizing the argument she herself used when hiring employees, Liss studied him with sudden suspicion. "Are you, by any chance, trying to teach me another lesson here?"

"What lesson would that be?"

"I thought you didn't believe in giving people a chance."

"I don't believe in giving people jobs they aren't suited for," he said. "But sometimes you have to take a chance. Speaking of taking chances . . ." He took her hand in his. "I'd like to suggest taking Mary Lee off waitressing."

"I'm not sure she can do anything else." She'd been expecting this particular conversation.

"She's a terrible waitress. How much worse can it get?"

"I won't fire her, if that's what you have in mind."

"If that was what I had in mind, you can be damned sure I'd say so."

She eyed him with skepticism. "No more hedging?"

"It's not really in my nature. Believe it or not, I'm a very forthright kind of guy. When I say I want something, I really want it." He hooked an arm around her waist, pulling her closer.

Liss's pulse went into overdrive. "What are you doing?"

"Being forthright. I definitely want you, Liss. And I want Mary Lee doing something where she can't spill water on anybody."

Liss took a deep breath and let it out again. "Have I pointed out to you that you have a very bad habit of making a pass at me every time you think I'm going to balk at something?"

He kissed her forehead. "Are you going to balk at reassigning Mary Lee?"

Liss sighed. "No. None of my customers have a death wish, that I'm aware of. She could probably act as hostess."

Josh rubbed his nose against hers. "Are you going to balk at having the students do the renovating?"

She shook her head. "No. Better them than me. I was afraid you'd think it would be good experience for me as a restaurateur to do it myself."

"Would I do that?"

"That's the whole point of this, isn't it? To give me experience? To make me see the errors of my ways and learn to be more self-sufficient?"

"I could teach you a number of things, if you'd let me," Josh said in a husky voice that made Liss almost forget that she was mad at him.

"In the bedroom and out of it, no doubt," she said dryly, though her heart was starting to pound as his hips settled against hers.

"I hate to disappoint you," he said, "but I'm not the sex maniac you seem to think I am."

Liss couldn't quite disguise her disbelief. "No?"

"No. In fact, there are any number of times I've wanted to throw you down on the floor and make hot, passionate love to you, and I haven't."

"How many times?" Liss asked, knowing if she insisted on playing with fire, she was going to get burned.

Josh pressed his lips against her forehead. "More times than you could count."

"I don't know," she said, reveling in the warmth of his body, so close to hers. "I can count pretty high."

"You wouldn't be teasing me by any chance, would you?"

"Does it sound like I'm teasing?"

"What it sounds like is that you've taken my exhortation to 'take some chances' to heart. Be good," he scolded as she purposely drew a line down the front of his shirt with her forefinger.

She smiled up at him. "If you're going to be bossy, I think you should know that I hate being bossed around."

"Were you this much trouble for Ray?"

"No. I was much more trouble for Ray. I'm taking it easy on you, because you obviously don't have much experience with assertive women."

"Are you now?" Mimicking her, he traced a line from her chin to her navel. "Anything else you want to know about my plans, you being an assertive woman and all?"

Liss stopped his hand before he could go any lower. "As a matter of fact, yes. I want to know when we're going to discuss the menu. I know you've got changes in mind, you being a self-avowed renovator. I'd like to know what they are so I can get myself a prescription for tranquilizers before you lower the boom."

"I'll tell you what I have in mind for changes after

you and I go furniture shopping," he promised. "Until then, don't go tugging on any tigers' tails. Taking chances is good," he added, stepping away from her with obvious effort. "You just want to live to tell about them."

TWELVE

If they lived to tell about their day together furniture shopping, Josh reflected the next afternoon, it would be a minor miracle. Liss had insisted on stretching his patience, and his self-control, to the limit. She'd been alternately irritating and seductive, when he couldn't do a damn thing about it, all day. Even though he knew she was doing it to get even, it still got to him.

It had started before they'd even left her place. He suggested, since they'd used his car for their wine-tasting trip, that they use hers to go furniture shopping. He'd figured it was a pretty good suggestion, especially considering she might insist on driving again. She obviously didn't see it that way.

"You want to use *my* car?" she asked, looking at him as though he'd just suggested they hotfoot it to Vegas to get married.

"Is there some problem with using your car?" he asked. He was determined not to let her light his fuse no matter how hard she tried.

"Yes."

"Are you going to tell me what it is?"

"Are you insisting on a reason?"

"No, I'm just asking if you have one. And since you apparently do, I just thought you might like to tell me what it is."

"I can't." She shook her head, swinging her soft blond hair from one side to the other.

"Why not?"

"Because you're going to think it's just one more thing we have in common, when anyone with any brains could see that we're nothing alike, that's why not."

Josh considered her remark, even as he contemplated touching her hair, running the silky length of it through his fingers. . . .

Stopping in midthought, he tried to figure out how her not wanting to use her car could have anything to do with him thinking they had things in common.

"What kind of car is it?" he asked, taking a stab in the dark.

She hesitated, his first clue that he was on the right track. "A Porsche."

"You drive a Porsche?" he asked, unable to hide his disbelief.

"No," she said, "I own a Porsche. I haven't driven it in quite some time."

Trying to get used to the idea of sassy but sensible Liss Harding driving a sports car, Josh studied her flushed cheeks. "Why the hell not?"

"Because it needs repair, that's why the hell not."

"Why don't you get it fixed?"

"Because I can't afford to. And," she added with

obvious reluctance, "because it's hard to get parts for it."

It took Josh a minute to make the mental leap. When he finally did, it was all he could do not to pull her into his arms and kiss her into tomorrow. "This wouldn't happen to be an older-model Porsche, would it?"

Liss's nose twitched in obvious consternation. "Yes. And you can stop smiling like that, because it doesn't mean what you think it does."

"Yes, it does." Josh couldn't help smiling in delight. "You like vintage sports cars, the same way I do. Where is it?"

She eyed him sourly. "In my garage."

"I want to see it."

It took him another ten minutes, and a fair amount of blustering and threatening to publish the damning review on the Lakeview—which was turning out to be a whole lot more useful than he'd first realized, considering he'd never intended to publish it in the first place—but he finally got her to unlock the one-car garage. Inside, hiding under a faded blue cloth cover, was a bright orange Porsche 911 in almost mint condition.

"This wasn't Ray's, was it?" Josh finally thought to ask. From the way her gray eyes took on a soft glow of adoration upon seeing the car, probably for the first time in ages considering the dust on the cover, he was pretty sure it wasn't.

"No," she admitted, looking like she wanted to touch the car, but was afraid to look too enamored with a machine. "It's mine. Ray liked his cars newer, and bigger."

Something in her voice made Josh ask quietly, "Did I hit a sore spot?"

She took a deep breath and let it out again. "Ray didn't like me owning the Porsche."

"Why not?"

"He didn't think women should drive sports cars."

"Because they're dangerous?" Josh had tried to form a picture of Ray, and of Liss's marriage to him, and came up blank every time.

"No, because he thought it made a woman look loose."

"That's ridiculous," Josh said, running his hand over the glossy orange surface of the right fender.

"That's what I told him. We had a running argument for months."

But she obviously hadn't gotten rid of the car. Which meant, either she was used to opposition from Ray, and had decided to ignore his objection, or that the car meant too much to her to acquiesce. Or maybe both.

Josh opened the driver's door and peered inside. "Do you miss him?" he asked, watching her out of the corner of his eye.

"Ray?" She hesitated only a second. "Sometimes."

He was surprised by her honesty. He'd halfway expected her to answer, "of course."

Pleased she trusted him enough to be truthful about Ray, especially when she knew he wanted her himself, and especially since she was still angry at him, Josh was silent, hoping she'd continue.

"That surprises you," she said after a moment. "Doesn't it?"

Afraid he was going to reach out for her if she gave him any encouragement at all, Josh slowly turned to face her. "A little. I thought you loved him very much."

She leaned against the car. "I did. He was a major part of my life for three years."

Trying to read between the lines, trying to decipher what it was she wasn't telling him, Josh reached for her hand. She let him take it reluctantly, but she didn't fight him. "Why do you sound bittersweet?" he asked.

She took a deep breath and let it out again, taking her time, as if deciding whether she wanted to discuss Ray with him. "Because I can't help wishing I'd done things differently. Better. With Ray."

"You and he got along, didn't you?"

She shrugged. "Most of the time. We didn't have a perfect marriage. There were times when I could've been easier to live with. There were times when Ray could've been more sensitive."

Josh brought her hand to his cheek. "Am I like him?"

"In some ways. He was darker. More volatile. But you and he have the same tendency to always think you're right."

"I am always right," Josh deadpanned. As Liss smiled wryly he feigned offense. "What's so amusing?"

"You are. That's the one big difference between you and Ray."

Josh kissed her palm and was pleased to see her eyes flicker with emotion. "What's that?"

"Ray was always so serious, so sure he knew the best, and only, way to do things."

"I thought he was a daredevil."

"He was a risk taker," she corrected him. "He

liked calculating the odds, then seeing if he could stretch things to the limit. In most situations, he was very predictable. If he thought he could get away with something, he did it."

"Am I that predictable?"

"You're predictably unpredictable. You keep me constantly off balance. Sometimes you seem bitter. Other times you refuse to take things seriously. It's like being on a roller coaster in the dark. You never quite know what's coming."

Josh softened his voice. "Do you like roller coasters?"

"I didn't used to." She sounded flustered as he played with her fingers. "I'm not sure anymore."

"Can I take that as encouragement?"

Liss raised both eyebrows at him. "I thought you took everything as encouragement."

He shook his head, grinning. "Ask a simple question, get an impertinent answer. Have I told you that you're a very sassy woman?"

"Repeatedly. Have I told you you're a very confusing man?"

"I was beginning to get that message." He kissed her fingers. "What else am I?"

"Well, you're bossy."

He kissed her wrist. "What else?"

She sucked in her breath as he traced her veins with his tongue. "You're recalcitrant."

He kissed the inside of her forearm. "What else?"

"Opinionated."

Moving closer, Josh kissed the inside of her elbow. "And . . . ?"

"Cagey," she said, shivering as he trailed kisses up to her bare shoulder.

"How about persistent, charming, and hard to forget?" he teased as he nibbled her shoulder.

"That too."

"Does it bother you?"

She didn't answer. Instead she managed to pull away as he tried to extend his exploration to the soft curve of her throat. "You're not coming on to me because you covet my car, are you? Because it's not for sale."

He smiled down at her, trying to look disarming. "It's a beautiful car. May I sit at the wheel?"

Looking piqued that he'd neither denied nor confirmed that his interest was on her car and not on her, she inclined her head, indicating her consent.

Sliding behind the steering wheel, Josh inhaled the pungent aroma of leather mingled with the dusty odor of neglect.

"This is too beautiful a machine to let it just sit here like this," he scolded.

"I don't have much choice," Liss said. "I'm too broke to get it fixed."

"You spent all your cash buying the car?"

"No. I've had the car since my twenty-first birthday. It was a present from my maternal grandparents. I was a classic-car buff long before I could drive. So was my grandfather. This was his."

"Then how come you're so broke? You don't strike me as a spendthrift, the type who shops till she drops. Not the way you were so reluctant to come with me today."

"Maybe I just don't like shopping for furniture," she said.

"Then again, maybe you're broke because you've put all your cash into the Lakeview." When she didn't deny it, Josh slid his palms over the leather-wrapped steering wheel, eyeing the controls with longing. That was better than eyeing Liss with longing and scaring her away. "This is probably an indelicate question, but what about Ray's life insurance?"

Liss pulled her hair over her shoulder. "Ray didn't have any. When he was single, he didn't think he needed any. After we got married and started up the restaurant, he just didn't have time to think about it."

"You mean he took the chance it would never be needed," Josh said gently, beginning to suspect she'd had a lot tougher time surviving the past year than she was willing to admit. "And you lost."

She lifted her shoulders in a negligent shrug. "I have the restaurant. It keeps me too busy to think about what might have been."

"How much do you like the restaurant business?" he asked. She'd more or less told him starting up the Lakeview had been Ray's idea. Ray's baby. "Be honest, now."

She hesitated. "I enjoy cooking. It's the managing part I don't much care for. I don't think I was ever meant to be a supervisor. And don't even begin to think what I think you're going to think," she warned.

He gave her an innocent look. "What's that?"

"Me cooking and you managing. Because it would never work."

"Have I suggested anything of the kind?"

"No. You just have that look again. It would never work," she repeated. "You and I don't agree on enough things to make it work, even if I wanted to go that route, which I don't."

"Ah, speaking of routes . . ." Pleased that she hadn't sounded too convincing in her argument, because the idea of sharing the responsibility for running the Lakeview with her had just filtered into his mind, Josh climbed out of the Porsche. "I have a few places in mind that we could check out for antiques. I thought I'd run them past you."

"I don't care where we go," she said, too casually to be believed, "or what you insist on showing me. I don't know anything about antiques."

"You don't have to know anything about antiques. All you have to do is agree with me if I tell you I think a particular piece would look great at the Lakeview." Josh smiled at her. "And we'll get along just fine."

They got along like a finicky feline and an oversized bulldog, Josh reflected later. Mostly because Liss insisted on needling him. Even though he knew she kept thinking, as he did, of their last day trip together, and what had happened at the end of it, she clearly hadn't yet forgiven him his trespasses, and had no intention of letting him think she had.

Amused by her recalcitrance, and both frustrated and bemused by her determination to pretend they'd never been intimate, Josh insisted on taking her to one antique shop after another. Not that it mattered. She disapproved of everything he liked. Still, he persevered, but was glad when they reached the last store he'd intended to visit.

"That's too big to fit in the foyer," Liss said as he showed interest in an enormous buffet.

"Not if we knock out a couple of walls," he said. When she narrowed her eyes at him, he lifted his hands in surrender. "It was a joke."

"Your humor is terrible," she said, skirting around an old trunk when he tried to take her by the elbow.

"And so is your taste in furniture. It's too big, too bulky."

"I suppose it's a little large for the foyer," he said, wishing she'd stand still so he could hold her. Kiss her. Make love to her. "But it would look great between the two windows facing east. And it would give the waiters and waitresses a place to put the sugars and creamers and such."

Halting suddenly, Liss raised an eyebrow. "I don't have any waiters."

"Well, not yet. They don't start until next week."

Liss stared at him. "Are you telling me, in your own peculiar, convoluted way, that you've hired one or more new employees without even bothering to consult me?"

"If I'd asked your opinion on hiring some new help, would you have said yes?"

"No."

"That's why I didn't ask." He gave her one of those "I'm so reasonable" looks she was beginning to distrust in the extreme. "Change is always difficult," he told her consolingly.

"Men are difficult in general, and you are difficult in particular," she retorted. "What if I don't like the new waiters?"

"You'll like at least one of them. It's Rob, your brother-in-law."

"How did you get him to agree to be a waiter?" She'd been trying for months to get him to take a more regular role at the restaurant, to no avail.

"I bribed him. What did you think?"

"What did you bribe him with?" she asked, almost afraid to know.

"Freedom from guilt. I told him you were having a

nervous breakdown brought on by stress from trying to do too much, and he could help by taking on some responsibility at the Lakeview. He's going to be head-waiter and assistant manager so you don't have to work eighty hours a week."

Liss sniffed. "I wasn't even close to having a nervous breakdown until I met you."

"You weren't having much fun, either," Josh said. "All you did was work, work, work. And every preschooler knows that all work and no play makes Liss a tired girl."

"I suppose you think it's fun looking around junk shops?"

Shifting his attention to a tile-topped table, Josh smiled in obvious satisfaction. "Damned right I do. Don't you?"

Actually, she did. At least, she did with him.

She'd never been a garage-sale sort of person, mostly because, even though people she knew always found bargains, she always found nothing but junk. But prowling around old antique-filled barns with Josh had turned out to be an educational, entertaining experience.

He seemed to have an unerring instinct for finding the one valuable piece in a pile of rejects. Half the things he'd shown her that day alone were real gems. The oak church pew was perfect for the foyer, and she thought the sideboard they'd snatched up was absolutely lovely. Not that she'd told him that. He seemed to think he could just tromp into her life and take over. Liss thought he had another think coming.

Consequently, she refused to agree with anything he said, and made a point of criticizing just about everything he wanted to buy.

"I'll tell you what," he finally said, when she'd disparaged his latest selection, the tile-topped table made of light oak. "You buy what I suggest, and we'll store your old pieces in the barn out behind my place, so if you decide you still want them, you can retrieve them."

"What if all this drives me out of business?" Liss asked. "Have you ever considered that?"

"New furniture never drove anyone out of business."

"Then why change?"

"Because your current decor will do nothing to increase, or keep, your business. Sometimes you have to change to stay the same."

Liss sighed. So far she'd been protesting on principle, but when he insisted on being reasonable, it took the wind right out of her sails and made her realize how very much she liked him. How very much she wanted to be close to him, in body and spirit, if she wasn't still so peeved at him.

Desperate to keep him at a distance, she reverted to the subject guaranteed to raise his ire and put him in anything but a reasonable mood.

"I suppose that you use this sort of cockamamie reasoning when you scuttle a restaurant's chances for being successful."

His long silence almost made her retract the stinging statement. "So, we're back to that, are we?"

"I wasn't aware that we'd ever gotten away from it." Knowing she was trying to irritate him to lessen the chance of them ending up in bed again, which they would if he didn't stop looking at her the way he was, Liss forged on. "You like taking control. You're a control freak. It must make you feel very powerful knowing you can make, or break, a restaurant with just words printed on a piece of paper."

"They aren't 'just words,'" he said politely, though she could see her remark had stung.

"No, you're right." She nodded in feigned agreement. "A lot of them are lies. Sort of like the one you told me. But whatever gets you the results you want, obviously will do."

Josh's mouth tightened in annoyance. "You're angry at me now. But later you'll see that I never meant to hurt you."

"I suppose you never meant to hurt any of the owners of the restaurants you've reviewed, either."

"That's right."

"I don't believe you."

"I know." He tied the small oak table—which he'd bought in spite of her objections—onto the top of his car. "That's why you're coming with me tonight."

She watched him knot the cord around the table. "Coming with you where?"

"To review the Village Inn in Penn Yan."

"Why would I want to do that?"

"To see if you can, of course." His smile was silky. "You know, I'm beginning to think that we need an addendum to our deal."

"What deal?" she asked suspiciously.

"The one where you wanted me to take over running the restaurant so I'd have egg on my face, of course."

She gave him a cool look. "I didn't want you taking over my restaurant. I just wanted you to experience what it's like to have someone taking potshots at you when you're trying to do your best."

"That's why we're changing the deal. I want you

to experience what it's like to do your job and have someone take potshots at you when all you're trying to do is your best."

Liss studied him, trying to decide if he was serious. "You actually want me to *review* a restaurant?"

"No." He tweaked her ear, sending a flurry of heat through her veins. "I insist on it. You wanted me to see how hard it is to run a restaurant. I want you to see how hard it is to fairly critique a restaurant. I'm doing your job, you do mine. If you can."

She scowled at him as he tested the table on top of his car for stability. "I'm not coming."

"If you don't come," he said, looking like he knew exactly how she'd take his remark, "I'll feel forced to use my original review of the Lakeview."

Liss seriously considered tying the cord around his neck. "Have I mentioned the word blackmail before?"

"What's the matter, Liss? Are you afraid you might not be able to stay angry at me if reason comes into this?"

"Reason and you are not two things I associate together."

"Do you associate us together?"

"No," she lied.

"Then there's no problem with you coming with me tonight, is there?"

There were all sorts of problems with the idea. For one, Josh might manage to convince her he wasn't a villain.

For another, she might end up forgetting how mad she was at him and start thinking about how much she liked him.

So, he could talk until he was blue in the face. She wasn't going to go with him, no matter what.

THIRTEEN

"What do you think of the filet of sole?" Josh asked as Liss cut into her dinner with all the relish of someone supplied with her last dinner before execution.

The mesquite-grilled fish was delicious, she thought. Not that she had any intention of telling him that.

Purposely vague just to goad him—after all, he'd shown up at her door, without warning, at six and all but dragged her with him to the Village Inn—she shrugged. "It's okay."

She wished she could say the same thing for herself. She'd been ridiculously nervous all evening. She'd dressed, putting on a simple black sheath and low patent-leather heels, with butterflies in her stomach. And now she was almost beside herself with anxiety.

What was he up to? Seduction? And if he was, would she succumb? Lord knew, she was in love with the man. She didn't want to be, but she was.

She watched as he poured her a second glass of chardonnay. "Do you like the wine?" he asked.

Again she shrugged. "It's okay." She had to force herself not to smile when he looked as though he could cheerfully throttle her.

"And the potatoes Lamartine?"

She looked down at the creamy chive-and-cheddar potatoes, which were apparently one of the specialties of the house.

Refusing to admit that they were heavenly, and done to perfection, as was the filet and the green beans, and everything else she'd sampled that evening, she gave another shrug. "They're okay."

"What do you think of the restaurant's environment?" Josh looked ready to get physical if she said "it's okay" one more time.

Hating to be predictable, Liss shivered. "It's over-air-conditioned. I'm freezing."

"And the help? How would you describe them?"

"They all seem a little surly, but," she added in a cheerful chirp she was fairly sure he'd take exception to, "the decor has a nice, authentic nineteenth-century flavor." Which it did. The faux gas lamps and furniture reproductions lent a pleasant historic feel to the atmosphere.

"And what do you think I'd say about the place?"

She smiled sweetly at him. "That it's got all the ambience of a wet basement and that its potatoes are pedestrian?"

"That's what I thought you'd say."

She knew she was in trouble when he smiled and showed her his notes, which he'd finished before he'd pumped her for her own opinion. Liss quickly skimmed them and discovered that his comments about the food were similar to her own unspoken ones.

No, not similar. They were exactly the same as hers.

Speechless, Liss sat back and looked at him. She'd honestly thought he enjoyed taking a restaurant down a peg or two. Enjoyed the power he held over the restaurants he reviewed.

But clearly, if this was really his true opinion, and not just something he'd done to impress her, he was trying to balance his more critical remarks—and there were quite a few of them—with a bit of understanding. For every uncomplimentary comment, he'd made a suggestion for improvement. It was constructive, not destructive, criticism.

And it was something she'd been thinking he needed to learn. Something she'd been trying to teach him. It appeared he'd taken her comments to heart. He was trying to balance the good with the bad. To make something positive, instead of something negative, out of the review.

More important, Liss knew he was trying to show her he'd changed.

Feeling her anger at him finally sliding away, she focused on her glass of wine and acknowledged that if she was still frightened of getting involved with him, it was no longer because she didn't know who he was or what he did. She was afraid because she still wasn't sure they were compatible. She didn't know what he wanted, from her or from life. And she didn't know whether he'd try to change her, as Ray had.

"If you were trying to be fair and not annoying," she asked, trying to sound unconcerned, just in case she wasn't as able to take criticism as she thought, "how would you critique the Lakeview?"

One dark eyebrow rose at her question. "The truth?"

"The truth," she said with a firm nod.

"I'd say the food wasn't bad, but the choice of entrées, and the presentation, could use a little rethinking."

It wasn't as deflating as she'd feared. Feeling encouraged, she asked, "What would you suggest for improvement?"

Josh tucked his pen back into the pocket of his navy blazer. "Considering your clientele, I'd stay away from high-priced French cuisine. Add some interesting dishes set at a moderate price. Salads with more than just iceberg lettuce and tomatoes. A little more flair in the appetizers. A little more adventure in general. Dining out should be an experience, not just an opportunity to fill one's stomach."

Taken back by his firm conviction, Liss paused. "You were involved with running a restaurant at some point in your life, weren't you?"

"You've already asked me that."

"I know I did. I don't recall you answering, you being in your secretive mode at the time. Have you ever worked in a restaurant? Yes? Or no?"

"Yes."

She blinked, thinking she might have a little trouble getting used to this instant access to information, once he'd gotten done with his obligatory teasing. "In what capacity?"

"I owned one."

Taken back once again, Liss noted that he'd used the past tense. "Where?"

"New York City."

"What happened to it?"

"My ex-wife got it in our divorce settlement."

She hadn't known he'd been married. Obviously not happily married. And she knew, without any doubt whatsoever, that the restaurant was what he'd given up without a fight and still regretted. The thing he'd hinted at that evening in her kitchen.

"I'm sorry," she said.

"Are you?" He eyed her with curious interest. "Why?"

"Because the restaurant obviously meant a lot to you. And you lost it."

"It was hard at the time." He leaned forward and captured her hand in his. "But I learned a lot from the experience."

Liss felt an immediate warmth surge through her at his touch. "What's that?"

"Never to let something important to me go."

Liss felt her heart start to pound. "Are we talking about anything in particular here?"

"I'm talking about you. And me. What we have together."

"Had," she said automatically.

"Have." His voice was low. "If you don't believe me, come outside with me now where we can have a little privacy and I'll show you."

"Lust doesn't make for a relationship," she said.

"No." His look sent her blood rushing like quick-silver through her veins. "It doesn't. It adds spice to one. As long as it's between the parties involved," he amended, "and not an outside party."

Liss felt her whole body come alive as he laced his

fingers with hers. "Was it an outside party that ended your marriage?"

"You're awfully nosy," he chided, squeezing her hand.

"I figured as long as you're answering questions, I ought to throw a few more at you while I have the chance. You might not be so willing to talk another time. So, was it some outside party that ended your marriage?"

Still holding her hand in his, Josh picked up his wineglass and took a sip. "In a manner of speaking. It was the restaurant that came between us."

"Because you got too bossy?"

"No, because I started liking it better than I liked Moira. I started spending more time with the restaurant than I did with her. A lot more. It was a more satisfying experience all around. Before long, she started getting resentful. Getting her hands on it when we separated gave her a lot of satisfaction."

"She made a huge success of it on her own?" Liss guessed. "Without your help?"

"No, she ran it into the ground. It closed less than six months after she took over."

Which obviously still bothered him. Liss could almost feel his pain, the regret burning inside him. "What makes you think the same thing wouldn't happen to us?"

Josh considered her. "For one, the Lakeview isn't mine, it's yours, so I don't have an emotional stake in its success or failure. For another, you aren't Moira."

Which was apparently good, Liss thought, and asked in what ways they were different.

"Moira was sophisticated, worldly, and very independent. She was a strong-minded, strong-willed woman. You, while being sassy as the dickens, are sweet, generous, and caring. I don't think you have a mean or selfish bone in your body."

"You make me sound like I have as much backbone as a jellyfish," Liss said, fearing that maybe he didn't know her as well as he thought he did.

"You care about people." His voice was gentle as he reached across the table and took her other hand in his. "Moira never really cared about anybody but herself. I have a tendency to be a little too cynical. You give me hope for the world. I hope I give you something in return."

He did. He helped her see things much more clearly.

She'd always had a tendency to be a little too emotional, especially when it involved people, and his reason and rational thinking set the world a bit straighter for her.

"But you already want to change the Lakeview," she argued, approaching the subject that still bothered her. "What if you start becoming more interested in making a success of the Lakeview than you are interested in being with me? The restaurant will end up coming between us, just like yours did with you and Moira."

"It'll never happen," Josh said with total conviction.

"Why not?"

"Because nothing could interest me more than you, that's why not."

Liss felt herself flush at his intensity, his sureness. "And what about my car?"

His thumb gently caressed her palm. "What about it?"

"You aren't going to deny you're interested in my Porsche. For all I know you want it as much as me and this is your way of getting it."

"I'm interested in *driving* it," he said, "not spending my life with it. Trust me. I'd take you over a machine any day." He smiled in bemusement. "You're not really worried about me wanting you for your car, are you?"

"I'm worried about you trying to take over my life. And possibly my restaurant. I don't want to lose the Lakeview."

How could she explain that she owed it to Ray to keep the restaurant going? To not let it fail?

Josh gave her hands a gentle squeeze. "Trust me. You won't lose the Lakeview, certainly not to me. And not to anyone else, if you're willing to take some advice about how to improve it."

"You're that sure you know what's best?"

"I'm that sure." His slow smile made her whole body go warm, from her nose to her toes. "And here I thought you didn't worry."

"I'm not a worrywart. I'm understandably concerned."

He shook his head. "If you say so. Look at it this way. I'm not exactly a novice in the restaurant business. And I'm not lacking comparisons. I've eaten in more restaurants in the past six months than most people try in a lifetime. And I haven't just wandered in and sat down and eaten. I've looked at them with a critical eye, with an eye for detail, with an eye for what needed to be changed and improved. I know what works and what doesn't. And I make a habit of talking to other patrons to see what they like and don't like and why. What they'd like to see changed."

Liss bit her lip. "I didn't know that."

"I didn't expect you to. I try to be fairly subtle about it. I bring things up in casual conversation while I'm waiting to be seated, in the cocktail lounge, wherever I think people might naturally shoot the breeze. And I use what they tell me to round out my reviews and reflect more than just my opinion. I talked to at least half a dozen people eating at the Lakeview. Do you want to know what they said?"

"I'm not sure," Liss said. "Am I likely to be upset?"

"That depends, I suppose, on how open-minded you are. Most of them liked the Lakeview."

"But?" she prompted.

"But they generally thought the atmosphere was a little stodgy, and the food could use a little more zip."

Trying not to take offense, because she knew he was right, Liss let out a long sigh. "I suppose you went and agreed with them?"

"No. I told them I thought the owners were trying to do their best with what they had. And that, with a small infusion of money and a little encouragement, the Lakeview could be a top-notch restaurant. You haven't been balking because you think Raymond wouldn't have liked things changed, are you?" he asked when she didn't immediately speak.

Liss looked over her glass of wine at him. "His name wasn't Raymond," she said. "It was Ramon."

Josh appeared bemused. "I guess that's why I can't seem to recollect ever hearing about him before. It's been driving me nuts. I've been racking my brain, trying to remember any mention of Raymond Harding."

This time it was Liss's turn to look disconcerted.

"His name wasn't Harding. That's my maiden name. I took it back after he died. Ray's last name was Villeaux."

Josh went so still, Liss thought at first she'd accidentally kicked him under the table or offended him in some way. Then, almost in slow motion, he sat back in his chair and looked at her with an expression she couldn't even begin to identify. "Your Ray was Ramon Villeaux?"

Puzzled by his reaction, she nodded. "That's right."

"The chef at Pierre's in Ithaca for a time?"

"He worked there for a couple of years," she said tentatively, not sure of Josh's mood. "Before we decided to open the Lakeview."

"He was a great chef."

"I know." She frowned. "Did you know him?"

Josh's mouth twisted. "I reviewed Pierre's once when I was upstate visiting my folks. The food was outstanding, but the atmosphere seemed a little tense. I seem to recall the chef chastising everyone around him in fluent, colorful French. I hear he did the same with my review."

Liss fiddled with her wineglass. "Ray resorted to his native language when he was exasperated." Which was much of the time with her.

Josh didn't seem to notice her hot cheeks. "He was from France?"

"Montreal. Rob was his half brother. He grew up in the U.S." Liss still felt embarrassed whenever she thought of Ray's French-Canadian heritage. Mostly because it had been his accent that had made her fall head over heels in love with him in the beginning. Of course, she'd been young and impressionable back then. "You don't speak French by any chance, do you?" she asked.

She was going on the theory that forewarned was forearmed. If Josh figured out she was a sucker for a French accent, who knew what he'd do to seduce her?

He shook his head. "I speak a little Spanish. That's all."

"Good."

He raised an eyebrow. "Why is that good?"

"No particular reason."

Josh signaled for their waitress. "So Ramon Villeaux started up the Lakeview. I think I'm beginning to see why you've been intimidated as a cook. And why you've been so reluctant to change things. Villeaux would be a hard act to follow."

"Does this mean you're going to leave my restaurant alone from now on?" Liss asked hopefully.

"Hell, no. You know me. I'm a man who loves challenges."

His smile was as wicked as the day was long. Consequently, when he drove her home, all Liss could think about was what he'd meant by that, and how the night was going to end.

Would it be with them together, in bed? Did she want it to?

She wasn't sure what she wanted, truthfully. She hadn't quite adjusted to not being mad at him. She'd been so certain she'd never see his point of view, that it would be easy to shoot down anything he said to justify what he did. But she couldn't.

She didn't know if that meant he was just a good salesman, or if it meant she loved him too much to see things in perspective.

She especially didn't know if it was wise to let

herself get any more physically and emotionally involved with him, until she knew what his intentions
were.

But even if she was confused, she was fairly sure
that making love was what Josh had in mind. He'd
been looking at her all evening like he could devour
her. She figured he'd drive her home, walk her to her
door, and ease himself inside before she knew what
was happening.

He surprised her, though. For one thing, he didn't
drive her home. At least, not her home.

"Where are we going?" she asked in confusion as
he turned the Corvette onto a narrow, winding road
leading down to the lake.

"My place."

She studied his neatly chiseled features in profile.
He looked perfectly at ease. Perfectly composed. Not
at all like a raving sex maniac, intent on ravishing her.

"Why are we going to your place?" she asked as he
tucked the car between two large maples and cut the
engine.

He turned to her, his face shadowed in the dying
light. "I want you to see where I live. How I live. I
don't want there to be any more secrets between us.
There's no need to be nervous," he added, tugging on
her earlobe. "I'm not going to have you for dessert."

"Do I look nervous?"

"You look ready to bolt out of the car. I wouldn't if
I were you."

"Why not?"

"There's about a fifteen-foot drop down to the
lake less than ten feet away."

"In which direction?" she asked coolly, not sure

she approved of the fact that he wasn't taking her home, and hadn't even asked if she minded.

"That's for me to know." He smiled at her look. "I'm teasing. I don't want you running off into the dark with some notion that I'm about to ravish you in a hot frenzy of desire."

"You don't plan to ravish me in a hot frenzy of desire?"

"Well." His smile shocked her down to her toes. "Not without your permission." He shook his head as her eyes widened in alarm. "Lord, you're easy to tease. Come inside, Liss. Nothing, and no one, least of all me, is going to harm you."

"This isn't going to be one of those lessons about why I should take a few more risks, is it?" she asked as he escorted her out of the car.

"No, it's going to be one of those lessons about why you shouldn't judge people until you really know them."

Liss was thinking that she *did* know him. And then she entered the cozy cottage he apparently called home.

Looking around the half-renovated structure, with studs in the walls still exposed in some places, Liss took a deep breath and realized he was right. She *had* been judging him on who she thought he was. What she thought he was.

Right from the beginning she'd decided he was a sophisticated man from New York City, with expensive tastes in clothes, and women for all she knew, who drove an old sports car because he like flaunting convention. A man experienced in the ways of the world, a man who had a way with women.

Judging from the cost of his clothes and his

penchant for choosing the most expensive items on any menu, while she habitually chose the least expensive, she'd halfway expected him to live in some sweeping cathedral-ceilinged cedar home, with floor-to-ceiling window walls, expensive leather couches, and a high-tech kitchen. She couldn't have been more wrong.

The wooden couch with cream-colored cushions looked new, but it also looked handmade by some local craftsman. And though the kitchen was well stocked and had decent appliances, it was anything but high-tech. Woven hangings covered some of the walls, exposed pipes decorated others. The only halfway luxurious amenity was a large, screened deck off the main living area, overlooking the lake.

"I'm still renovating," he explained as Liss looked over her surroundings in disconcerted silence.

He'd said he was a born renovator, almost the first time she'd met him. But she'd never realized that bent extended to everything from houses to restaurants.

Still worried that his interest in her might be entangled, even confused, with his interest in the Lakeview and that it would fade once the renovations were finished, Liss studied the rough wooden floor, afraid if she looked at him, he'd know what she was thinking.

"You didn't build it, then?" she asked, trying for the life of her not to sound as upset as she felt. What if that was all that it was? What if his interest really was focused on making over the Lakeview, and she just happened to be the owner? Someone who amused him, maybe. Had caught his interest in a very temporary sort of way.

"I like taking things that need help, giving them care and attention, rebuilding them and watching them become successes. It's more interesting than starting from ground zero. The cottage was a burned-out shell when I got my hands on it."

"But renovating is a lot of work," she pointed out. She, too, liked remolding things, and people, and watching them become successes. "And there are no guarantees it will be good as new, or better than new, when you're through."

"I enjoy the process of making things over. Salvaging them."

Afraid he was going to say something like that, Liss plunged on. "But what about when you're done? Don't you feel restless for new challenges?"

"Sometimes. Sometimes it's nice to just revel in a job well done for a while."

Which would it be with the Lakeview? And her? Would he want to rest on his laurels and revel in a job well done when he was through? Or would he lose interest and want to move on? Losing interest in both the Lakeview and her.

"You look deep in thought." He reached out and caught her hand. "Come sit out on the swing with me. Watch the sun set."

The sun had almost disappeared below the horizon, the sky emblazoned with red and gold, the lake a shadowed presence in the foreground.

Led out through the sliding-glass doors onto the screened porch, Liss sat beside Josh on a large wooden swing hanging by chains from the rafters. Josh had obviously worked a lot on the cottage. Despite his claim that he hardly knew one end of a hammer from the other, he'd clearly put in plenty of hours and hammered more than a nail or two rebuilding it. There couldn't have been too much standing after the fire.

He'd put lots of effort into making a home for himself. Not to mention a fair amount of money.

She took a deep breath as he slid his arm around her and pulled her into the curve of his shoulder. After a moment she looked up at him. "Can I ask you something?"

He kissed her hair. "Ask away."

"Reviewing restaurants can't be a full-time job. So, I was wondering. . . . What else do you do?"

He brushed his lips against her hair. "I teach."

She couldn't hide her surprise. "You're a teacher?"

"At the vocational school in Flint."

"What do you teach?"

He smiled. "Restaurant management, what else?"

What else, indeed? At least teaching sounded stable. And long-term. Unless, of course, it was only a temporary position.

More confused than ever, Liss listened to the crickets chirp. Holding her close, Josh gave her a gentle hug, then leaned away. "I almost forgot. I have a present for you."

"You've already given me a bouquet of flowers tonight," she reminded him, thinking of the white and pink carnations he'd handed her when he'd picked her up earlier that evening.

"A person like you can't have too many presents," he told her, pulling a tiny package from his pocket.

Recognizing that she had yet to give him anything, except maybe grief, Liss reluctantly took it. "What kind of person am I?"

"Sweet. Sensible. Forgiving."

"I'm not so sure I've forgiven you," she said, although she knew she had. How could she not? The man was unbelievable. Persistent. Thoughtful. Sensitive. Kind. And confusing.

"That's why I'm giving you another present. Just in case."

She unwrapped the small package. It was a miniature skunk, holding a flower and a sign that said FORGET ME NOT.

"What am I going to do with you?" she muttered in exasperation.

"You could kiss me," Josh suggested. "As a token of thanks."

Afraid if she kissed him she'd want to do a lot more, Liss said firmly, "Just a peck on the cheek. As a token of thanks. That's all."

But, of course, it wasn't all.

The moment her mouth was within an inch of his cheek, he turned so their lips met. And the moment their lips met, their bodies were drawn toward each other like some immutable force of nature. Reminded all over again of the night they'd made love, Liss felt her heart slamming against her ribs.

Josh rested his hand on her nape. "God, you feel good," he murmured against her mouth.

So did he. He felt wonderful.

Knowing he wanted her as much as she wanted him, Liss waited for him to deepen the kiss. She tingled with anticipation as he explored one corner of her mouth, then the other, and she moved closer, hoping to banish her uncertainties in the heat of his embrace.

Instead, he slowly withdrew.

"What's wrong?" she asked, feeling bereft as he pulled away.

"Nothing." He took her hand and helped her to her feet.

"Then what are we doing?"

He brought her hand to his lips, brushing them against her soft skin. "I think it's time to get you to bed."

Surprised, not only by his bluntness, but by her instant reaction to the huskiness in his voice—her heart was racing and her knees felt weak—Liss said as firmly as she could, "I have no intention of going to bed with you until, or unless, our problems are resolved."

"That's good. Because I have no intention of going to bed with you until our problems are resolved, either."

She looked at him in deepening confusion. "You mean you're taking me home?"

"No, I mean I'm sleeping on the couch. You get my bed. It's king-size. You'll like it."

Wondering why he never did or said what she thought he would, Liss frowned at him. "You're not sleeping with me?" She wasn't sure if this was a good thing, or even if it was what she wanted.

"If I sleep with you," he said, "I'll want to make love to you. And if I make love to you, you'll end up thinking that I'm trying to sway you into agreeing with me, of not contradicting me, or challenging what I want to do with the Lakeview."

"You don't want me to agree with you?" she asked, wondering why she felt so hollow and so empty, knowing he wasn't going to make love with her. And that his unexpected decision was really for the best.

"I want you to express your honest opinion," he said, resting his hands on her waist. "So that in the end, the Lakeview is yours, not mine. I don't want you to have any regrets about the restaurant. Or about us." He pulled her throbbing body close enough to plant a kiss on her forehead, then with an effort she could feel, he held her away again. "The master bath is all yours," he said as he walked her to his bedroom door. "Help yourself to towels or anything else. I'll be on the couch if you need anything."

"What if I want you to make love to me?" she asked, shocked at herself, and dismayed by her voicing the confusion in her mind.

He kissed her on the tip of her nose. "Then you're out of luck, at least for tonight. I don't make love to confused women. Even beautiful, desirable ones."

"You think I'm confused?"

His smile made her stomach do a little flip. "I think you're irresistible. Beautiful. Desirable. Sassy and opinionated. And confused. You need time to sort things out. Decide how you feel about me. About us."

"What if I sleep alone tonight, and I'm still confused?"

"If you're still confused by this time tomorrow, we'll pursue this conversation. In the meantime try to get a good night's sleep. Because I'm going to be very trying tomorrow."

As Liss walked into his cream and navy-blue bedroom and closed the door behind her, she decided he was being trying already. And she doubted if she was going to sleep a wink knowing he was on the other side of the door.

FOURTEEN

Dragged out of a deep, troubled sleep as Josh knocked on the door, Liss sat up and pulled the dark blue sheets up to her chin. She took a deep breath, cleared her throat, and prayed for composure. "Come in."

The heavy pine door was pushed open on creaky hinges and Josh, looking disgustingly fresh and cheerful, ambled in. "Good morning, sleepyhead. Time to rise and shine."

Yawning, Liss pushed a hand through her tangled blond hair. "What time is it?"

"Five."

"*Five!*"

"I'm an early riser."

"You're crazy, that's what you are." She stifled another yawn and took the large mug of coffee he was handing her.

"Crazy about you." He smiled at her soft snort as he sat on the edge of the bed.

Aware of the warmth of his firm thigh pressing

against hers through the thin sheet and blanket, Liss inhaled the rich aroma of her coffee.

"This is wonderful. Thank you."

"You're welcome, Wart."

The cup stopped halfway to her mouth. "Did you just call me *Wart*?"

"It's my new name for you. As long as you're going to keep worrying about everything and acting like a worrywart . . . You're not going to throw that cup of coffee in my face, are you?"

"I'm thinking about it. I have no intention of being addressed as Wart," she told him, sipping gratefully at the coffee.

"I guess I'll have to come up with something else to call you. How about Nervous Nellie?"

"How about my name?" She swallowed another sip of coffee. "Are you trying to irritate me?"

"No," he answered, looking far more attractive than Liss thought he had a right to be, considering the hour. "I'm trying to get you to stop worrying so much. I'm also trying to figure out how that sign about not sweating the small stuff got put on your kitchen wall."

"That's easy. Rob put it there."

"I take it the sign was put there for your benefit?"

"I don't worry that much," she protested.

"You're worrying right now."

"No, I'm not—" She stopped talking when he shifted his weight, rubbing his thigh against hers.

He gave her a serene smile. "See?"

"Anyone would worry with you around," she said in self-defense.

He leaned closer, planting a hand on the bed near her hip. "What is it you think I'm going to do?"

Liss automatically leaned back in a vain attempt to put some distance between them. "Take advantage of me, me being in a state of dishevelment and not quite awake."

"If I'd wanted to take advantage of you," he said, "I could have done it during the night when you were completely defenseless. You're a very heavy sleeper, aren't you?"

She raised a quelling eyebrow even as she reveled in his closeness. "And just how would you know that, if you were sleeping out on the couch?"

"I had to sneak in and get some clothes when I got up. You didn't even stir. I could've come in wearing combat boots and blowing a trombone and you wouldn't have woken up. You look like a twelve-year-old when you sleep, all curled up into a ball."

Wondering what would have happened if she *had* awakened, Liss eyed him warily. "Is that what you came in to tell me at five in the morning?"

"No, I came in to tell you it's time for hands-on experience."

"Your favorite kind," she murmured into her coffee cup.

"I heard that."

"You were supposed to." Liss finished the coffee and, feeling more invigorated, pushed her tousled hair out of her face. "You're not going to try to distract me all day by making passes at me, are you?"

"Fair is fair." He ran his finger down her cheek. "You distract the hell out of me just by breathing."

When she *could* breathe. Realizing the closer he got, the more trouble she was having taking in air, Liss said firmly, "I suppose I'd better tell you now, I have no intention of letting you take things over."

He touched the dimple in her cheek. "Are we talking about anything in particular here?"

"Me and the Lakeview, not necessarily in that order."

"You're still worrying about that, aren't you?" He shook his head. "You're afraid to let me in your life, afraid to let me get my hands on the business, because you can't shake the idea that I want to control things. Why? Is that what Ray did?"

Surprised by the question, Liss looked at him for a long time before answering. "Yes."

"I thought you two had a good marriage."

"We did."

"But he wouldn't let you participate in decisions involving the Lakeview, would he?"

She hesitated, then admitted, "No."

"And you think I'm cut from the same cloth."

"I don't know if you are or not. I just don't think I could handle another take-charge male in my life. I've grown used to doing things for myself. Making all the decisions. Being totally responsible, not just for myself, but for the restaurant."

"Fair enough." Josh rose and walked toward the door.

Tempted to follow him, until she remembered that she was wearing only her black bra and panties, Liss asked, "What does that mean, fair enough?"

He stopped at the door. His hand on the heavy pine slab, he looked back at her. "It means I'll bring up suggestions and you have the right to nix them if you don't like them. I'm not unreasonable."

"You're just saying that so I'll let you do what you want."

"No, I'm saying that because you're obviously in

need of reassurance. And because I mean it. If you don't want to change something, say so, and we won't change it."

"You weren't this amenable when it came to suggestions about furniture," she pointed out as he came back and sat down beside her again.

His slow smile sped up her heartbeat.

"I can't help it. I'm partial to oak." He leaned toward her, until his mouth hovered a millimeter above hers. "And you."

Liss tried to remember how to breathe. "Is this another pass?"

"What do you mean, another?" His lips touched hers in a light butterfly kiss. "I thought it was my first pass of the day."

But obviously not his last. He cupped her nape and urged her mouth closer to his, brushing his lips against hers again. Tantalizing. Teasing.

"You're a very funny guy," she murmured, melting under his touch.

"You're a very beautiful woman. And a very big worrywart about all the wrong things." He kissed her nose. Then her forehead. Then her cheeks. "What do you suppose we should do with each other?"

Trying not to think of what she wanted to do with him, Liss took a deep calming breath. "I'll bet you have a few suggestions."

"I've got all kinds of suggestions about all kinds of things. However . . ." Surprising her, he reached over to a nearby chair, grabbed a handful of clothes, and laid them beside her on the bed. "Right now I'd suggest you get dressed before I retract that promise not to make love to you while you're confused. You *are* still confused, I trust?"

"Very." It wasn't a lie. She *was* confused. About him. About them. And it didn't look like she was going to be enlightened about either one anytime soon.

He smiled and left her to get dressed. As soon as he'd exited the bedroom, Liss tugged on the sweatpants and oversized man's dress shirt. Two pieces of toast and a couple more cups of coffee later, she sat beside him as he drove them to the Lakeview.

Liss noticed with surprise that most of the furniture had been replaced already. New slatted-back oak chairs with dark blue padded seats dotted the room alongside the newly polished oak tables.

"Those look expensive," she said as she ran a finger over one of the chairs, enjoying the smooth texture of the wood.

"They weren't cheap," Josh said, pulling her closer. "But they were worth it. Quality lasts."

But would *they* last, Liss wondered, once they got down to the nitty-gritty of running the restaurant?

"So," she said, trying to be her usual optimistic self. "What do we do first?"

"Cook for me," Josh said as he handed her an apron.

Immediately suspicious as he proceeded to tie it around her waist, from the front, requiring him to put his arms around her, Liss focused on his cleanly shaven chin. "Is this some sort of audition?"

"If you want to call it that." He blew her bangs off her forehead. "But not, as you obviously suspect, for you. I want you to make some new dishes for me so we can decide, together, if they belong on your new menu or not."

Trying hard to be open-minded, Liss asked, "What shall I make?"

"Desserts?"

More comfortable with that suggestion than if he'd asked for zippy new appetizers or elegant main dishes, Liss considered him. "What kind?"

"How about apricot crêpes flambés?"

She raised an eyebrow. "Why? So you can tell me they taste like burned tires?"

"You're not going to let me live that one down, are you? Forget the crêpes. How about making me a cheesecake?"

"Which kind? Chocolate? Or pedestrian?"

He took the sarcasm without batting an eyelash. "Your choice."

Determined to show him she could take criticism and learn from it, Liss made her mother's blueberry-cheesecake recipe while Josh looked on.

"Suggestions?" she asked as he watched in silence.

His brown eyes met hers, and Liss saw the admiration in them. "Just one small one . . ."

She listened to his suggestion that she add more vanilla and a touch of almond extract. Conceding that he knew what he was talking about, Liss went along willingly with the changes Josh suggested in three more concoctions.

Well, more or less willingly. Confident enough of her own cooking talents when it came to desserts to let her own preferences be known, she couldn't help testing Josh to see if he was sincere about not insisting on his way all of the time.

"You're not being purposely contrary just to see how far you can push me, are you?" he asked, when she balked at making a minor adjustment in a chocolate-raspberry torte.

She batted her lashes at him. "If you can't take the heat . . ."

"Get out of the kitchen. I know." He slid his arms around her waist, oblivious to the smudges of flour and sugar on her apron. "You're not going to make this easy, are you?"

"You don't want it to be easy. You told me you like challenges."

"Did I? When?"

She stilled his hands as he started to undo the buttons on her oversized shirt. "When I was balking at letting you in my life. Or my restaurant."

"So I did." He turned his attention to her neck, kissing it. "What do you say we try a cake or two?"

She shot him a reproachful look over her shoulder as he tried to undo her bra. "What do you say you behave yourself?"

"I don't know how. I need you to teach me."

She let out a sigh as he explored the nape of her neck.

"I don't suppose you'd like to give me a hand in the kitchen, would you?" she asked, figuring busy hands were safer hands.

"I've been trying to give you two hands for at least the past two hours," he complained, "and you aren't having any of it."

"I meant in cooking."

"All right." He sighed and released her. She immediately perched on a stool while he turned to the stove.

He glanced at her. "I thought you wanted help."

"I do. I haven't got a clue where to start when it comes to pasta. I thought you might like to try something . . . exotic."

"I would. You."

"I'm not exotic," she said. "And you're not behaving. Again. Cook," she commanded. "Or I'm going to do something physical."

Josh smiled. "Promises, promises."

But he behaved. He was too busy to do otherwise. Liss watched him in amazement as he whipped up one dish after another, with all the finesse of an artist approaching a new canvas.

He winked at her. "Now for the finishing touches."

She watched in awe as he turned a radish into a rose in the space of ten seconds. Garnishing the series of colorful, appetizing plates, he set them on the counter in front of her and whipped off his apron. "What do you think?"

"I think Anthony is probably going to have a fit when he sees what we've done to his kitchen."

"He'll get over it. But you better have a fire extinguisher nearby for a while, just in case." Josh bent down and began sorting through the case of wine he'd brought up from the cellar while Liss had been concocting desserts.

"What are you doing?" she asked as he pulled out half a dozen bottles and set them on the counter.

"If we want to sell more wine, it's helpful to have a larger variety so that there's something to go with every entrée. I thought we might offer whites made in New York and reds from California."

"What's this 'we' business?" she teased, nibbling on a heavenly fettuccine Alfredo he'd stirred up in less time than it took her to wash and dry her hands.

He just grinned and pulled out a cabernet. "What do you say to this with the fettuccine?"

She shook her head. "It's red."

"So?"

"So you can't serve red wine with pasta with cream sauce."

"Why not?"

She rolled her eyes in exasperation. "I can't speak for the rest of the world, but I prefer a lighter wine with a cream sauce. I'd rather have a white zinfandel."

Josh dropped the cabernet back into the case. "Fair enough."

"Are you agreeing with me because you agree with me?" she asked. She thought he'd given in too easily. "Or because you want to have your way with me tonight?"

"I'm agreeing with you because it doesn't matter that much to me." He set down his plate of pasta. "And because I want to have my way with you tonight."

Liss felt her heart start to thump as he moved closer. "What is it, exactly, that you want to do with me?"

He showed her. Sliding his arms around her, he silenced her with a leisurely kiss that singed her down to her toenails.

"I really don't think we ought to be doing this here," she said breathlessly, when his mouth finally left hers.

"You're absolutely right." He immediately changed their location, dragging her into a hallway where he proceeded to kiss her again, just as thoroughly.

Liss sighed as he melded his body with hers after letting her up for air. "I suppose this is your way of compromising."

"That it is." He nuzzled her neck, sending her blood stampeding through her veins. "What's yours?"

"I was going to suggest the storeroom. Anthony and I are the only ones with keys."

Josh smiled as he nibbled her collarbone. "I like that suggestion."

She sighed again. "I suppose that's another compromise on your part."

"I'll tell you what I won't compromise on."

She felt her whole body start to throb as he explored the cleft between her breasts. "What's that?"

"You and me being alone, together, after we leave here."

Liss wove her fingers through his dark hair, holding him close. "And just what is it that you think we're going to do?"

"That's up for negotiation. But it had better involve a lot of touching, and a lot of kissing, or no deal." He kissed her soundly for emphasis.

Liss had hardly gotten her key out of the door after locking up for the night before he turned her around to face him.

"My place?" he asked. "Or yours? Just decide quick because a man can exercise only so much self-control."

"I don't know." She pretended indecision. "I'm a little confused . . ."

He kissed the smile off her face. "Things getting any clearer?" he asked huskily as she clung to him for support.

"My place," she managed. "It's closer."

"You're sure now?"

"Sure that it's closer?"

"No. Sure you want this."

"What's this?" she asked in feigned confusion, enjoying being in control, just for a little, even though her own body was clamoring for closer contact.

"Let me show you." He kissed her until she couldn't remember her name, then drove her home. Standing in the doorway, they paused to kiss in the dark. Holding her and kissing her until she was breathless, Josh refused to let her go.

Once inside, they didn't even bother to turn on the lights. They headed for her bedroom, entwined in each other's arms, their mouths melded in the heat of their passion.

Inside her bedroom, Josh kicked the door shut, his hands going to the buttons on her shirt. "You don't need to close the door. There's no one here," Liss told him, her breath coming in quick gasps as he swiftly undressed her.

"I'm not taking any chances." Josh heard the roughness in his voice and knew he was close to losing control. "I want you all to myself." He'd wanted her for ages. Wanted to love her. And be loved.

His hands smoothed the shirt over her shoulders and he felt his body physically aching for her. To be one with her.

"God, Liss." He buried his face in her fragrant hair, loving the feel of her skin. Her hair. Her mouth. He sampled all of her as he dropped her shirt to the floor, then moved his hands to the clasp on her bra. "You feel wonderful."

"You feel pretty good yourself," she whispered, her breath coming quick and uneven as he reached behind her.

"Pretty good?" He nipped her earlobe in rebuke.

"Damned good," she corrected herself, stifling a groan as he circled her ear with his tongue.

"Watch your langue," he scolded as he divested her of her bra. Then her jeans. Then her panties. "You're shocking me."

She shook her head. "No, I'm not. Nothing shocks you. That's one of the things I love most about you." She pressed up to his bare chest. "I can be myself around you. I don't have to pretend to be helpless. Or dependent."

"No more half-truths or evasions between us," he promised as he tugged off his own clothes and pulled her down onto the bed with him.

"Or clothes?" she asked, reveling in his maleness, his strength, as he rested his weight on her.

"Sassy woman," he said, sliding up against her softness. "What am I going to do with you?"

"Come closer," she said huskily, putting her arms around him, "and I'll give you a few suggestions."

Afterward, snuggled in Josh's arms, Liss reflected on what had happened. How she felt about him. How she felt about the two of them together. He wasn't the bulldozer she'd thought he would be. In fact, he was far more sensitive than she ever could've imagined. And although she wouldn't have thought so even a day or two ago, it looked like things were going to work out between them.

She loved him. He loved her. Even if they didn't always agree, and two opinionated people rarely did all the time, they'd learned to compromise. To talk and work things out.

Both of them had changed. Were changing. Josh

had learned to be more understanding and less critical. And she'd learned that she could be liberated and independent, and still accept help. And that just because a man liked being in control didn't mean he couldn't also compromise and share responsibility.

They were a lot alike, Liss realized, in all the ways that counted. So it was all the more surprising when all hell broke loose a few days later.

It happened when Josh indicated he wanted to make one last change at the Lakeview. The physical design of the menu.

Liss supposed she shouldn't have been surprised. After all, they'd already changed the inside of the restaurant, not to mention what was served. It was a natural suggestion, but a deadly one.

Aware that Josh had not only been supervising the building of the trellised patio, but had been hammering away himself for hours, Liss was standing at the front counter when Josh walked up to her.

Flicking on the antique lamp he'd helped her pick out, he draped an arm around her shoulders. "I have something to show you," he said, handing her a copy of the new menu.

From his manner, Liss knew he was expecting her approval.

She tried to maintain an open mind as she inspected the professional-looking menu, with a pen-and-ink drawing of the Lakeview on it.

"I commissioned a local artist to give it a new look," Josh said when she didn't immediately speak. "What do you think?"

Liss didn't know what to think. She should've seen this coming, she supposed. But since he hadn't brought it up, she'd put off thinking about it. For good reason.

She passed it back. "It's very nice, but I don't think so."

Clearly surprised, but apparently thinking she was joking, Josh handed it to her again. "Why not?"

"I can't." She passed it back again.

"Why not?" Josh repeated, holding on to it this time.

So upset she could barely speak, Liss shuffled papers near the register. "Because."

"Because why?"

She took a deep breath and tried to get her jumbled thoughts together. "You wouldn't understand."

"Why not?" he asked again.

"Because you just wouldn't, that's all."

"It's Ray, isn't it?"

Liss knew she should've expected that too. Goodness knew, she'd used Ray as an excuse whenever she'd been desperate to keep at least some control.

"What is it? Are you afraid that Ray wouldn't like it?"

Having no idea how to explain her feelings to him, Liss finally stopped shuffling papers and faced him. "I know you want what you feel is best. But you don't know how I feel."

"I know that you love me and I know that I love you. Nothing else is important."

"This is important," she insisted. "To me."

She could see him fighting to understand. "You don't want to redesign the menu?"

"It's not a question of wanting." She picked up the Lakeview's original menu, which was simple, even amateur, in comparison. "I can't just toss this."

"Why not?"

Fairly sure she was going to scream if he said "why not?" one more time, Liss finally confessed, "Because Ray designed it, that's why not."

"I see." Josh put his fists in his jeans pockets, but his gaze never left her face.

"What do you see?" she asked, not at all sure he understood since she wasn't sure she understood her emotions either.

Josh's voice was soft. And filled with regret. "I see that this is my fault. That I've been rushing you. It's only been a year, after all. Even so, I'd hoped you were over him. But you're not, are you?"

She felt her insides ache. "I knew you wouldn't understand."

"How can I understand when you won't talk to me?"

"You don't want me to talk to you," she said, desperately trying to think of a way to explain it to him. "You want me to agree with you. And I can't. Not on this."

She knew she'd hurt him from the way he studied her in silence. His voice was strained when he finally spoke. "I'm sorry you feel that way. I guess there's nothing else to say, is there? You obviously need more time, and more space." He leaned forward and kissed her on the forehead. "Take care of yourself, Liss." Then he turned and walked away, right out the door.

"What's wrong?"

Startled by the voice behind her, Liss turned to find Rob watching her with concern.

Filled with pain, she lifted her shoulders. "Nothing. Everything."

"Well, that made things a lot clearer. Let me make

a guess. Farrington wants something and you feel you can't give it."

"He wants to redesign the menu," Liss confessed, barely able to speak.

"And you said . . . ?"

"I said I couldn't."

"Why?"

Faced with Rob's obtuseness, Liss let out a sigh of exasperation. "You know why. It's the only thing left that was Ray's. We've changed the interior. We've changed what we serve . . ."

"You'd already changed what you serve," Rob pointed out reasonably. "It was one of the first things you did."

"Because of necessity. I couldn't cook the way Ray did. I'm not talented the way he was."

"And you don't think changing the menu design is a necessity?" He shook his head in bemusement. "I mean, Liss, look at it. I loved Ray. He was my brother. But he was no artist, and we both know it." He eyed her in silence a moment. "You know what I think? I think you're scared."

"Don't be ridiculous. What could I be scared of?"

"Of taking the final step. With the restaurant. And with Farrington." He paused a moment. "Would I be wrong in guessing that you wouldn't even discuss changing the menu?"

Liss hesitated. "I told him Ray designed it. That's it."

"And he naturally assumed that you not wanting to change it has to do with Ray, when we both know it has to do with Farrington. Tell me something. Do you love him?"

"No. Yes. I don't know—" She halted. Yes," she said finally. "I do."

"Are you willing to lose him over something Ray did—in one night, I might remind you—only because you two didn't have the money to have a professional artist do the menu in the first place?"

Liss took a deep breath, trying to imagine a life without Josh. Trying to imagine going back to the way things were. "I don't want to lose Josh," she said honestly. "He's the best thing that's ever happened to me." She stopped. "Not that Ray and I—"

Rob put a finger over her lips, preventing her from finishing. "I know how things were between you and Ray. You don't need to apologize. Or explain. Ray was something of a bulldozer. We both know it. That doesn't mean we didn't love him, but he didn't exactly go around asking our opinions about things. It was okay at the time. You and I were both young and inexperienced in the ways of the world. But since he died we've both had to grow up a lot. We had to take things over. Neither one of us is the same person he left behind. We were forced to make a lot of decisions when he died." Rob paused. "I think you need to make one now."

"What's that?"

"You need to decide whether or not you love Farrington enough to put away the past once and for all. Ray's not here. Farrington is."

"I didn't think you even liked him."

Rob smiled. "I didn't at first. I didn't like what I thought he was. But we both know you can't judge a book by the cover. And you can't judge the critic until you see past the job. Besides." He reached out and tweaked her hair. "The man's obviously crazy about you. He'd do anything for you."

Liss raised a skeptical eyebrow. "How do you know that?"

"Because he put not only his own time and sweat into your restaurant, he put his own money into it as well. If that's not love, I don't know what is."

"He did that," Liss pointed out dryly, "because he plans to take it over."

Rob shook his head. "He could've bought the Firestone, but he didn't. He could've bought the Dockside, and he didn't."

"He loves challenges," Liss said.

"He loves you," Rob answered back. "And you love him. I guess the only question is, what are you going to do about it?"

FIFTEEN

Knowing that Rob was right, Liss walked home in sheer misery that night. She still couldn't believe she'd allowed something like a *menu* to drive her and Josh apart. What was a menu, after all? Ink and paper.

Sitting on her couch, she studied the floor as she ran her hand over the dark blue material of the sofa cushions, and she suddenly knew exactly where to go. And what to do to correct the situation. She had to find Josh. She had to talk to him. If he was still talking to her.

Grabbing her keys, she tromped into the garage, determined to get her recalcitrant car going if she had to kick it. But to her surprise, it started on the first try. Not sure she trusted the vehicle, even if it did seem to be running so smoothly it practically purred, she drove at a snail's pace down to Josh's cottage to talk to him. Parking the Porsche, she walked up to the front door and knocked. Once. Twice. No answer.

Refusing to give up, she walked around to the back

of the cottage, where she spotted his neatly tended herb garden. And his equally tidy flower garden.

Spying the colorful vase of blooms through the screened-in porch, Liss shook her head in amazement. Josh was clearly a man who not only planted flowers, but who picked them and put them on his dining-room table. And she'd thought he was insensitive?

More determined than ever to see him and make amends, she tried opening the back door, expecting it to be locked. It wasn't.

Easing it open, she called out. No answer. Feeling curiously at home, rather than an interloper, she wandered around the living room, noting with bemusement what she hadn't seen before. He collected miniature animals, just as she did.

Curious to see the rest of the house, since Josh hadn't given her a tour the night she'd stayed over, Liss went into his study. From the look of the desk, it was fairly obvious this was where Josh worked. The tidy desk didn't surprise her, but the awards did. Stuffed high and low on bookshelves, but not displayed, were numerous certificates and trophies. Some, she noted, were culinary awards, but others were for charitable works. Random kindnesses.

Feeling her heart ache, Liss walked back out into the living room, and knew she'd been wrong about him. He wasn't the uncaring, unjust man she'd originally tried to convince herself he was. On the contrary, he was probably twice as sensitive and caring as any man she'd ever met. Certainly more selfless than she'd given him credit for. And she'd probably lost him.

On her way outside, she noticed that his recycling bins near the back porch were full. An empty wine

bottle caught her eye. It was an unusual label for a
local winery, Sapphire Hills. Not one of the wines
they'd bought during their wine tasting trip.

Pulling it out, she studied the label. The drawing
was nicely done, in the same style as the new design
Josh wanted for the Lakeview's menu. Puzzled, she
turned the bottle around and read the print on the
back.

There was nothing extraordinary. The usual stuff
about how the wine came to be made, and then, at the
bottom, was the winemaker's name and signature.
John Farrington.

John *Farrington*!

Stunned, Liss realized it had to be a relative of
Josh's. Possibly his father? He'd mentioned that his
father had once owned a winery. He'd also mentioned, she'd thought jokingly, that he was going to
bring his mother to the Lakeview, when he was trying
to talk her into renovating.

But it had never occurred to her that his family
lived locally.

Going back to her car, Liss dug out her map of the
area, the one that showed where the wineries were.
She found the words *Sapphire Hills* where she least
expected it, and swiftly realized they'd practically been
sitting in his family's vineyards when they'd had their
picnic after their wine tasting.

Sneaky devil, she thought admiringly.

There was always something unexpected to discover about him. Always some new surprise awaiting
her.

Liss decided to come up with a surprise of her
own.

She drove to the winery, and sure enough, the

house just up the hill from it had the name Farrington on the mailbox. Parked in front was Josh's black Corvette. An addition to the winery was three quarters finished, with a sign announcing COMING SOON. THE TERRACE CAFÉ.

Gathering up her courage, not sure what she was going to say or do, only certain that she had to see Josh, she rapped lightly on the door.

A tall, handsome woman in her fifties, with Josh's eyes and a feminine version of his mouth, opened the door.

Liss extended her hand. "Hi. I'm Liss Harding." She smiled, nervous and trying to hide it. "You must be Mrs. Farrington."

"Call me Jayne." A warm smile greeted her. "Liss, it's so nice to finally meet you."

Finally? "You know who I am?" Liss asked in surprise.

"Lord, yes. I've been hearing about you ever since Josh met you. I've hardly heard him talk about anything else for days." She swung the door open. "Come on in, dear. If my motherly instincts are operating properly, you two need to do some talking."

"Why would you think that?" Liss asked as the other woman closed the intricately carved door and ushered her into an enormous terra-cotta-tiled foyer.

Jayne Farrington looked amused. "Because one, you don't look like the kind of woman who usually comes to a man's parents to introduce yourself. And two, because Josh has been looking like someone kicked him ever since he arrived about an hour ago. And three, because he and his father have been sitting out on the deck for the past half hour discussing the dangers of fraternizing with headstrong women. I think they're sympathizing with each other. Much good it will do them," she added with a conspiratorial wink. "If they'd wanted wimpy women, they should have gone after wimpy women. And since they haven't . . ." She paused, then asked, "What has Josh told you about me and his father?"

"Josh said you were a little opinionated," Liss said, almost apologetically, "but I thought he was just teasing because I was balking at renovating the restaurant."

"Liss, dear. You haven't a clue what opinionated is until you've lived with a Farrington male for a decade or two. You should know that before you get married to one. Are you and Josh likely to marry?" she asked, clearly not the least bit hesitant about the subject.

"I'm not sure," Liss said, "but I think it's a distinct possibility."

"Good." She smiled in approval. "You look like just the woman to handle him. He was always a recalcitrant child."

Returning the other woman's smile, Liss walked beside Josh's mother to the deck overlooking the winery and the lake.

Shooting a nervous look at Josh, who'd risen at their entry and was watching her with caution, she smiled as she was introduced to his dad. John Farrington had risen, too, and was looking her over with obvious approval. "Looks like an opinionated woman to me, son," he decided, grinning.

"She is, Dad," Josh said. "Damned stubborn."

"Do you love her?"

"Yes, Dad. I'm afraid so."

"What are you going to do about it?"

"Marry her, Dad. If she'll have me."

Liss looked from Josh to his dad and back again. "Are you two going to stand there and talk about me like I'm not even here?" she asked.

Josh's dad smiled even more broadly at her. "We like to live dangerously, we Farringtons. Welcome to the family, Liss." He gave her a quick hug, then excused himself, along with Josh's mother, and left the two of them alone.

Josh leaned back against the deck rail, watching her for a moment. "How did you know where I was?" he finally asked.

"I snooped around your cottage. It's a good thing you're a committed recycler, or I would've been left without a clue." As he frowned in puzzlement she explained, "The wine bottle. I went through your trash."

"Ah." His smile was faint but amused. "That was sneaky."

"I was desperate."

"A desperate woman. My favorite kind."

"I'm also exasperated. How come you never suggested your family's winery when we were looking for wine for the Lakeview?"

"Because I didn't want you to know who I was then."

"But later, after I knew . . . ?"

"I wanted to put off bringing you here. I was afraid you'd see that I was building a restaurant of my own and maybe start thinking I geared my reviews to eliminate the competition. Or worse, you'd see me as competition. You already seemed intimidated by living in Ray's shadow. I didn't want you thinking you had to stand in mine. Besides"—his mouth twisted—"my folks are a little muleheaded. They tend to scare people off."

"I'm used to muleheaded people," Liss told him. "In fact, I'm partial to muleheaded men."

"Are you, now. Why?"

"I love challenges."

He smiled. "Do you?"

"I also love you."

"You're not just saying that because you want something from me, are you?"

"I'm saying that because it's true. And," she added, "because I want something from you."

"And what's that?"

"A chance to talk things out. I like your folks," she added, when he didn't immediately speak again.

"The way you and Mom came out here, I got the feeling you'd become instantaneous friends. So what did my mother tell you about me?"

"That you were recalcitrant as a child and nothing much has changed since. I think I could agree with that assessment."

Josh took her hand and urged her closer. "Were you hoping to change me?"

"No." She felt her chest tighten. "I like you just the way you are."

"Do you, Wart? I like you just the way you are too." Pulling her against him, he kissed her, savoring her mouth, the taste of her. Finally lifting his head, he ran his hand down her hair, smoothing it. "Can we compromise on this problem with the menu?"

She turned her head so his hand brushed her cheek. "What would you suggest?"

"How about celebrating the old, instigating the new?"

"I don't understand."

"We could frame the old menu and put it in a prominent spot on the wall in the foyer, and use the new design for everyday. I was thinking maybe we should rename the restaurant while we're at it."

Knowing he'd said it just to see how she'd react, Liss gave him a considering look. "What would you suggest?"

"How about Ramon's?"

She felt as if her heart would explode. "You'd do that?"

He brushed the tendrils of blond hair lovingly from her face. "I'd do anything to make you happy."

"In that case . . . I think we ought to call it Joshua's."

"You'd do that?"

"I'd do anything to make you happy," she said, knowing she'd learned the most important lesson of all: That sometimes, even while you treasure the past, you have to let it go.

Josh smiled then, pulling her close until their bodies were melded. "Then why don't we compromise and just keep calling it the Lakeview? I've always liked the name."

She swayed against him. "I have another question for you."

"You want to know where my money came from."

She looked up at him in surprise. "How did you know?"

"Because if you started writing out checks to me, I'd want to know the same thing."

"So are you going to tell me? Or do I have to guess?"

"I'm embarrassed to tell you. Moira's dad was

some big shot on Wall Street. He'd always taken a liking to me, even if his daughter grew to despise me."

"He gave you a few suggestions and you made some money on the stock market," Liss guessed.

"No." Josh rested his chin on her head. "He gave me a few suggestions and I made a lot of money. An embarrassingly large amount. It seems only right to make good use of it. Goodness knows, I didn't do anything to earn it."

"You amaze me," Liss said.

"Sometimes I amaze myself. Especially when I act dumb. There was no excuse for me keeping the truth from you for so long."

"Don't worry about it." She wrapped her arms around his waist. "I'm planning to make you pay for it for years."

"Speaking of plans . . . I have some for the future we need to discuss."

"What are they?" she asked, reveling in the feel of him, wanting to be still closer.

He just smiled. "You'll see. . . ."

The salad was two forks, and even that was being generous.

Holding up her lettuce-laden fork, Liss looked at Josh across the small table. "What exactly is *in* this salad dressing, anyhow?" she asked, repressing a shudder.

Josh took another bite of salad. "Tastes like anchovy paste to me. The chef here is partial to it. God knows why."

Nodding, Liss took a tentative bite of her entrée. "How would you rate the whipped potatoes?"

Josh considered the potatoes, served in a hollowed-out orange with a serrated edge on top. "I'd give them a five for appearance but a three for taste. They've got lumps."

Liss nodded her agreement. "I hear they had some sort of power surge yesterday that fried some of their electric appliances."

"Ah." Josh reconsidered his judgment. "Then I'll give them a four for effort and I won't mention the lumps. Hand-whipped potatoes are okay for the family for Thanksgiving, but they're the dickens to do in quantity. What are you smiling at?"

"I'm smiling at you." Liss speared a wilted green bean.

"Why?"

"Because I love watching you work. It's like watching a modern-day Solomon. I've never seen anyone so intent on being excruciatingly fair."

He rolled a pearl onion across his plate. "Thank God I don't have to go around threatening to split babies in half to do the job. All I have to do is survive flaccid green beans and steaks that resemble shoe leather."

"Dick McGregor wouldn't have asked for your input," Liss pointed out, "if he thought everything was done as it should be. In any case, you'll like dessert. The chef specializes in chocolate amaretto cheesecake."

"How would you know that?"

She smiled at him. "I snooped in the kitchen."

"Speaking of desserts, I like watching you work as well."

"I thought it was the end product you liked."

"It's an added bonus. I think having you open a

coffee-and-dessert shop was inspired." He gave her a beatific smile. "I'm glad I thought of it."

Liss just rolled her eyes in amusement. After some intensive soul-searching she'd finally acknowledged that while she didn't want to lose the Lakeview, she didn't really enjoy managing it either. So she'd ended up asking Rob how he felt about taking over. Since Josh was building the Terrace Café, she'd hoped to leave the running of the Lakeview to Rob while she continued to do the desserts.

But within a month Josh, ever the renovator, had convinced her to build on a small adjoining café called "Just Desserts," where people could drop by for coffee and dessert. It was Liss's baby, and Josh was turning out to be her best customer.

But even after opening the Terrace Café, which served light sandwiches, along with Liss's desserts, he wasn't content to rest on his laurels.

Before long Josh suggested they form the Finger Lakes Restaurant Association, consulting with other eating establishments in the area, helping them become the best they could be, as well.

"I like your idea for having a 'heart healthy' charity cook-off for all the local restaurants," Liss said, filled with love and admiration for Josh's penchant for doing good deeds.

He shrugged. "It made money for a worthy cause and provided all the local chefs with the impetus to use their creativity. We all gain."

"Anthony stewed for a week, staying after closing, trying to come up with something original and healthy. I think it defeated him at first not being able to use cream and butter."

Josh grinned. "He looked like a nervous wreck

there for a while, but he came through in the end. His lentil chili deserved first place. Speaking of healthy cooking and not using cream and butter . . . I thought you calling the dessert portion of the cook-off 'Sweet Nothings' was inspired. I never knew nonfat mousse was possible, let alone so delicious." He raised a questioning eyebrow. "What are you thinking?"

She smiled. "I'm thinking you're wonderful. By the way, you wouldn't happen to know how my Porsche got fixed, would you?"

"Well . . ."

"Don't tell me, let me guess. Was it the fix-it crew from Flint?"

"Who else? When they realized the patio wouldn't take as much time as we originally thought, they offered their services. You should've seen them at work. They were something else."

"I think it's probably a good thing I didn't see them," Liss decided. "You didn't happen to hire them to work at our wedding next week, did you?"

Josh looked innocent. "Someone needs to provide the entertainment now that Mary Lee's gone off to college. Look at it this way. If anybody's car won't start after the ceremony, we've got the situation covered."

Liss shook her head. "You didn't also offer to give any, or all, of them employment after they finish their schooling, did you?"

"We'll all need more help if business keeps picking up the way it has been. And they needed encouragement. I figured they'd be more likely to complete their education if they were given incentive. Most of them are unbelievably stubborn and recalcitrant. Like you."

Liss sniffed. "You'd know what stubborn and re-calcitrant is. I never saw a man so determined to get his own way."

"I'd like to have my way with you. Right now. What do you say we go to a quiet place to discuss that?"

Liss felt her heart start to thump at his look. "I think we need to pay our respects to the owner and give him our critique first. He'll need time to straighten things out before the paper's new food critic decides to drop in. Are you planning any more random kindnesses in the near future?"

"I don't know about random kindnesses . . ." Josh's voice dropped to a husky purr as he captured her hand and brought it to his lips. "But I'm planning on plenty of random kisses."

Liss's eyes reflected the love shining in Josh's. "You're not trying to seduce me so I'll give you my secret recipe for cheesecake flambé, are you?"

His smile was as wicked as upstate New York winters were long. "Would I do that?"

"You're hopeless," she decided, smiling up at him as he helped her out of her chair.

"Hopelessly in love with you," he murmured in her ear.

And he always would be.

THE EDITOR'S CORNER

Prepare to be swept off your feet by the four sizzling LOVESWEPT romances available next month. Never mind puppy love—you're soon to experience the tumultuous effects of desperation and passion in this spring's roller-coaster of romance.

Bestselling author Fayrene Preston turns up the heat with **LADY BEWARE**, LOVE-SWEPT #742. Kendall Merrick trusts Steven Gant when she should be running for her life. From the moment they meet, she is certain she knows him—knows his warmth, his scent, and the heat of his caress—but it just isn't possible! Steven hints she is in danger, then tempts her with fiery kisses that make her forget any fear. Has she surrendered to a stranger who will steal her soul? Find out in this spellbinding tale from Fayrene Preston.

Change gears with Marcia Evanick's playful but passionate **EMMA AND THE HANDSOME DEVIL,** LOVESWEPT #743. She figures Brent Haywood will be happy to sell his half of Amazing Grace, but when the gorgeous hunk says he is staying, Emma Carson wonders what he could possibly want with a chicken farm—or her! Fascinated by his spunky housemate, Brent senses her yearnings, guesses at the silk she wears beneath the denim, and hopes that his lips can silence her fear of never being enough for him. Discover if opposites really do attract as Marcia Evanick explores the humor and touching emotion of unexpected love.

THICK AS THIEVES, LOVESWEPT #744, is Janis Reams Hudson's latest steamy suspense. Undercover agent Harper Montgomery stands alone as his brother is buried, remembering how Mike had stolen his future and married the woman who should have been *his* wife. Now, ten years later, Annie is no longer the carefree woman he remembers. Harper is determined to learn the bitter truth behind the sadness and fear in her eyes—and find out whether there is anything left of the old Annie, the one who had sworn their love was forever. Janis Reams Hudson fans the flames of reawakened love in this sizzling contemporary romance.

Join us in welcoming new author Riley Morse as we feature her sparkling debut, **INTO THE STORM,** LOVESWEPT #745. If all is fair in love and war, Dr. Ryan Jericho declares the battle lines drawn! Summer Keaton's golden beauty is true temptation, but the software she has designed will cost him a halfway house for kids he counsels—unless he distracts her long enough to break the deal. Scorched by a gaze that lights a fire of longing, Summer struggles to survive his seduction strategy without losing her heart. Riley Morse creates a pair of tantalizing adversaries in this fabulous love story.

Happy reading,

With warmest wishes!

Beth de Guzman   Shauna Summers
Senior Editor   Associate Editor

P.S. Don't miss the exciting women's fiction Bantam has coming in June: In **FAIREST OF THEM ALL,** Teresa Medeiros's blockbuster medieval romance, Sir Austyn of Gavenmore, in search of a plain bride, wins Holly de Chastel in a tournament, never suspecting her to be the fairest woman in all of England; Geralyn Dawson's enticing new charmer, **TEMPTING MO-RALITY,** has Zach Burnett conceiving a plan to use Morality Brown for his personal revenge—only to have the miracle of love save his soul. Look for a sneak peek at these dazzling books in next month's LOVESWEPT. And immediately following this page, look for a preview of the terrific romances from Bantam that are *available now!*

Don't miss these extraordinary books
by your favorite Bantam authors

On sale in April:

DARK RIDER
by Iris Johansen

LOVE STORM
by Susan Johnson

PROMISE ME MAGIC
by Patricia Camden

"Iris Johansen is one of the romance
genre's finest treasures."
—*Romantic Times*

DARK RIDER

by the *New York Times*
bestselling author

IRIS JOHANSEN

New York Times *bestselling author Iris Johansen is a
"master among master storytellers"* and her bestselling
novels have won every major romance award, including the
coveted* Romantic Times *Lifetime Achievement Award.
Now discover the spellbinding world of Iris Johansen in her
most tantalizing novel yet.*

*From the moment she heard of the arrival of the English
ship, Cassandra Deville sensed danger. But she never expected the sensuous invader who stepped out of the shadows
of the palms and onto the moonlit beach. Bold, passionate,
electrifyingly masculine, Jared Danemount made it clear
he had every intention of destroying her father. But he
hardly knew what to make of the exquisite, pagan creature
who offered herself to him, defiantly declaring that she*

* Affaire de Coeur

*would use his desire to her own advantage. Still, he could
no more resist her challenge than he could ignore the temptation to risk everything for the heart of a woman sworn to
betray him.*

"Are you truly a virgin?"

She stiffened and then whirled to face the man
strolling out of the thatch of palms. He spoke in the
Polynesian language she had used with her friends,
but there could be no doubt that he was not one of
them. He was as tall but leaner and moved with a
slow, casual grace, not with the springy exuberance of
the islanders. He was dressed in elegant tight
breeches and his coat fit sleekly over his broad shoulders. His snowy cravat was tied in a complicated fall
and his dark hair bound back in a queue.

*He is very beautiful and has the grace and lusty appe-
tite of that stallion you love so much.*

Her friend Lihua had said those words and she
was right. He *was* beautiful. Exotic grace and strength
exuded from every limb. High cheekbones and that
well-formed, sensual mouth gave his face a fascinating
quality that made it hard to tear her gaze away. A
stray breeze ruffled his dark hair and a lock fell across
his wide forehead.

Pagan.

The word came out of nowhere and she instantly
dismissed it. Their housekeeper Clara used the term
to describe the islanders and she would deem it totally
unfit for civilized young noblemen. Yet there
was something free and reckless flickering in the
stranger's expression that she had never seen in any of
the islanders.

Yes, he must be the Englishman; he was coming from the direction of King Kamehameha's village, she realized. He probably only wanted supplies or trade rights as the other English did. She did not have to worry about him.

"Well, are you?" he asked lazily as he continued to walk toward her.

He might not be a threat but she answered with instinctive wariness. "You should not eavesdrop on others' conversations. It's not honorable."

"I could hardly keep from hearing. You were shouting." His gaze wandered from her face to her bare breasts and down to her hips swathed in the cotton sarong. "And I found the subject matter so very intriguing. It was exceptionally . . . arousing. It's not every day a man is compared to a stallion."

His arrogance and confidence were annoying. "Lihua is easily pleased."

He looked startled, but then a slow smile lit his face. "And you are not, if you're still a virgin. What a challenge to a man. What is your name?"

"What is yours?"

"Jared."

"You have another name."

His brows lifted. "You're not being fair. You've not told me your name yet." He bowed. "But, if we must be formal, I'm Jared Barton Danemount."

"And you're a duke?"

"I have that honor . . . or dishonor. Depending upon my current state of dissipation. Does that impress you?"

"No, it's only another word for chief, and we have many chiefs here."

He laughed. "I'm crushed. Now that we've established my relative unimportance, may I ask your name?"

"Kanoa." It was not a lie. It was the Polynesian name she had been given, and meant more to her than her birth name.

"The free one," the Englishman translated. "But you're not free. Not if this person you called the ugly one keeps you from pleasure."

"That's none of your concern."

"On the contrary, I hope to make it very much my concern. I've had very good news tonight and I feel like celebrating. Will you celebrate with me, Kanoa?"

His smile shimmered in the darkness, coaxing, alluring. Nonsense. He was only a man; it was stupid to be so fascinated by this stranger. "Why should I? Your good news is nothing to me."

"Because it's a fine night and I'm a man and you're a woman. Isn't that enough?"

LOVE STORM
by Susan Johnson

"Susan Johnson is one of the best."
—*Romantic Times*

Desperate to avoid a loathsome match, Zena Turku ran from the glittering ballroom in the snowy night and threw herself at the mercy of a darkly handsome stranger. He was her only hope of escape, her one guarantee of safe passage to her ancestral home in the Caucasus mountains. But Prince Alexander Kuzan mistook the alluring redhead for a lady of the evening, the perfect plaything to relieve the boredom of his country journey. Only after her exquisite innocence was revealed did the most notorious rake of St. Petersburg realize that his delicious game of seduction had turned into a conquest of his heart.

Zena experienced a frightening feeling of vulnerability when this darkly handsome prince touched her; it was as though she no longer belonged to herself, as though he controlled her passion with his merest touch.

The prince must think her the most degraded wanton to allow him such liberties, to actually beg for release in his arms. A deep sense of humiliation swept over her as she tried to reconcile this astonishing, unprecedented sensuousness with the acceptable behavior required of young society debutantes. How could she have permitted these rapturous feelings of hers to overcome her genteel upbringing? Certainly the prince would never respect her now.

Zena's eyelashes fluttered up and she gazed surreptitiously from under their shield at the man who had so casually taken her virginity. He was disturbingly handsome: fine, aristocratic features; full, sensitive mouth; dark, long, wavy hair; smooth bronze skin. The brilliance of a huge emerald caught her eye as his hand rested possessively on her hip, making her acutely aware of the contrast between their circumstances. He was handsome, rich, charming, seductively expert, she ruefully noted. Plainly she had made a fool of herself, and her mortification was absolute. But then she reminded herself sharply that *anything* was superior to having to wed that odious toad of a general, and the prince *was* taking her away from St. Petersburg.

The emerald twinkled in the subdued light as Alex gently brushed the damp curls from Zena's cheek. "I'm sorry for hurting you, *ma petite*," he whispered softly. "I had no idea this was your first evening as a streetwalker. Had I known, I could have been more gentle."

At which point Prince Alexander was presented with some fascinating information, most of which he would have quite willingly remained in ignorance of.

"I'm not a streetwalker, my lord."

Alex's black brows snapped together in a sudden scowl. *Bloody hell, what have I got into?*

"I'm the daughter of Baron Turku from Astrakhan."

The scowl deepened noticeably.

"My father died six months ago, and my aunt began trying to marry me off to General Scobloff."

The frown lifted instantly, and Alex breathed a sigh of relief. At least, he mentally noted, there were no irate relatives to reckon with immediately. "Sweet Jesus! That old vulture must be close to seventy!" he exclaimed, horrified.

"Sixty-one, my lord, and he's managed to bury two wives already," Zena quietly murmured. "I didn't want to become his wife, but my aunt was insisting, so I simply had to get away. My little brother and I will—"

"Little brother?" Alex sputtered. "The young child isn't yours?" he asked in confusion, and then remembered. Of course he wasn't hers; Alex had just taken her virginity! A distinct feeling of apprehension and, on the whole, disagreeable sensations struck the young prince. *Merde!* This just wasn't his night! "You deliberately led me on," he accused uncharitably, choosing to ignore the fact that he had drunk so much in the past fifteen hours that his clarity of thought was not at peak performance.

"I did not lead you on!" Zena returned tartly, angry that the prince should think she had contrived this entire situation. "Modest young ladies of good breeding do not lead men on!" she snapped.

"Permit me to disagree, my pet, for I've known many modest young ladies of good breeding," Alex disputed coolly, "a number of whom have led me on to the same, ah, satisfactory conclusion we have just enjoyed. They're all quite willing once the tiresome conventional posturing has been observed."

The prince's obvious competence in an area of

connoisseurship completely foreign to Zena's limited sphere served to squelch her ingenuous assertion.

Alex sighed disgruntledly. *Good God, for which of my sins am I paying penance?* "What am I to do with you—a damnable virgin? Of all the rotten luck! You try to be helpful and come to the aid of what appears to be a nice, ordinary streetwalker and look what happens. She turns out to be a cursed green virgin with a baby brother to boot, not to mention a respectable family."

"No, my lord, no family," Zena quietly reminded him.

A faintly pleased glint of relief momentarily shone in the depths of the golden eyes. "Thank God for small favors. Nevertheless, you, my dear, have become a vexatious problem," Alex censoriously intoned.

"You could take the honorable course of action and marry me, my lord."

PROMISE ME MAGIC

by the extraordinarily talented

Patricia Camden

"A strong new voice in historical fiction . . . This is an author to watch!"
—*Romantic Times*

With a fury born of fear, Katharina had taken aim at the bandit who dared to trespass on her land and fired only to discover that the powerful warrior she felled was a man she thought long dead . . . a man who had stolen her fortune . . . a man she despised. Now, as she gazed into Alexandre von Löwe's smoldering gray eyes and felt the overpowering pull of his attraction, she wondered why she'd let the scoundrel live and how she was going to tell him she was masquerading as his wife. . . .

"I am Katharina von Melle," she told him, then waited as if expecting a response.

"Madame von Melle," he said, giving her a slight nod. He grimaced and bit back a ripe oath. Someone had just lit the powder touchhole of the cannon in his head.

"Katharina," the woman gritted out as if to a slow wit. "Anna. Magdalena. von Melle."

Obviously, she thought he should know her. A

OFFICIAL RULES NO PURCHASE NECESSARY

To enter the sweepstakes outlined below, you must respond by the date specified and follow all entry instructions published elsewhere in this offer.

DREAM COME TRUE SWEEPSTAKES

Sweepstakes begins 9/1/94, ends 1/15/96. To qualify for the Early Bird Prize, entry must be received by the date specified elsewhere in this offer. Winners will be selected in random drawings on 2/29/96 by an independent judging organization whose decisions are final. Early Bird winner will be selected in a separate drawing from among all qualifying entries.

Odds of winning determined by total number of entries received. Distribution not to exceed 300 million. Estimated maximum retail value of prizes: Grand (1) $25,000 (cash alternative $20,000); First (1) $2,000; Second (1) $750; Third (50) $75; Fourth (1,000) $50; Early Bird (1) $5,000. Total prize value: $86,500.

Automobile and travel trailer must be picked up at a local dealer; all other merchandise prizes will be shipped to winners. Awarding of any prize to a minor will require written permission of parent/guardian. If a trip prize is won by a minor, s/he must be accompanied by parent/legal guardian. Trip prizes subject to availability and must be completed within 12 months of date awarded. Blackout dates may apply. Early Bird trip is on a space available basis and does not include port charges, gratuities, optional shore excursions and onboard personal purchases. Prizes are not transferable or redeemable for cash except as specified. No substitution for prizes except as necessary due to unavailability. Travel trailer and/or automobile license and registration fees are winners' responsibility as are any other incidental expenses not specified herein.

Early Bird Prize may not be offered in some presentations of this sweepstakes. Grand through third prize winners will have the option of selecting any prize offered at level won. All prizes will be awarded. Drawing will be held at 204 Center Square Road, Bridgeport, NJ 08014. Winners need not be present. For winners list (available in June, 1996), send a self-addressed, stamped envelope by 1/15/96 to: Dream Come True Winners, P.O. Box 572, Gibbstown, NJ 08027.

THE FOLLOWING APPLIES TO THE SWEEPSTAKES ABOVE:

No purchase necessary. No photocopied or mechanically reproduced entries will be accepted. Not responsible for lost, late, misdirected, damaged, incomplete, illegible, or postage-die mail. Entries become the property of sponsors and will not be returned.

Winner(s) will be notified by mail. Winner(s) may be required to sign and return an affidavit of eligibility/release within 14 days of date on notification or an alternate may be selected. Except where prohibited by law entry constitutes permission to use of winners' names, hometowns, and likenesses for publicity without additional compensation. Void where prohibited or restricted. All federal, state, provincial, and local laws and regulations apply. All prize values are in U.S. currency. Presentation of prizes may vary; values at a given prize level will be approximately the same. All taxes are winners' responsibility.

Canadian residents, in order to win, must first correctly answer a time-limited skill testing question administered by mail. Any litigation regarding the conduct and awarding of a prize in this publicity contest by a resident of the province of Quebec may be submitted to the Regie des loteries et courses du Quebec.

Sweepstakes is open to legal residents of the U.S., Canada, and Europe (in those areas where made available) who have received this offer.

Sweepstakes is sponsored by Ventura Associates, 1211 Avenue of the Americas, New York, NY 10036 and is represented by independent businesses. Employees of these, their advertising agencies and promotional companies involved in this promotion, and their immediate families, agents, successors, and assignees shall be ineligible to participate in the promotion and shall not be eligible for any prizes covered herein. SWP 3/95

And don't miss these electrifying
romances from Bantam Books,
on sale in May:

FAIREST OF THEM ALL
by bestselling author
Teresa Medeiros

"Teresa Medeiros writes rare love
stories to cherish."
—Romantic Times

TEMPTING MORALITY
by award-winning author
Geralyn Dawson

"[Geralyn Dawson] weaves a deliciously
arousing tale."
—Affaire de Coeur

"von Löwe," she called, nudging him again. "Colonel, there's one thing you should know before we reach Löwe Manor."

He grunted, drifting back into oblivion.

"I'm your wife."

Alexandre woke up.

"You may stay until Tragen has recovered enough to travel. But you must give me your word that Löwe is mine."

He sucked in a breath of victory. "You have it."

"Say the words."

"I give you my word that Löwe Manor will be yours."

"Not will be . . . *is!*" She moved around to where Alexandre could see her, and what he saw made him go still inside. Distrust, despair, and an iron will to go on. It was the look of a woman touched too closely by war. He'd seen it before, on other women's faces, on those who had survived.

"Löwe is yours," he said softly.

"And . . . and you must accept whatever you find there."

He narrowed his eyes. "Why? What will I find there?" She did not answer. "What will I find there, Kat?" Silence. He let his head fall back to the folded wool, but through his lashes he could still see the black point of the pistol barrel aimed at him. "I will accept whatever I find there . . . within the restrictions of my oaths to the emperor, the duke of Tausend, and my men."

The gun barrel did not waver for a heartbeat. Then two . . . three . . .

"Cross me and you're a dead man," Katharina said with the tempered steel of conviction. And lowered the pistol.

He closed his eyes in relief. Whatever desperate hold he'd had on his awareness left him then, and he began to slip into sleep.

A nudge roused him to semiawareness. "Colonel

"Impossible."

"No, Colonel von Löwe, *possible*. In fact, more than possible. It has been done. A fait accompli. Löwe Manor is mine. For four years I have lived there, and no one has challenged me." A mixture of guilt and bravado flashed through her eyes, the same look a woman gets who has cheated on her lover and now seeks to deny it. He had barely registered that it was there before it was gone. She sighted again down the barrel of the pistol with renewed determination.

"And now, Colonel, though you neglected to give me a choice about my future when you stole my fortune from me, I shall give you a choice about yours. You can choose to leave—with Löwe remaining in my possession—or you can choose to contest my ownership. Of course, if you choose the latter, the hero dies, shot for a brigand on his way home. Such a shame."

"So the bastard daughter would turn murderer? Such a shame."

He heard her lick her lips. "You and Tragen and the other one can move to Alte Veste. It is but a day's ride from here."

"A day's ride straight up. It's coming on to winter, Kat . . . Katharina," he said carefully. "Alte Veste is deserted, and has been for three generations. Cold, too, and full of drafts. Tragen would probably succumb."

He waited, his breathing nearly suspended. He needed the obscurity that Löwe Manor could provide—at least until late February or early March. And after that, given von Meckler's delight in all things ravaged, they all would most likely be looking for a new place to live. If they were still alive.

middle, from the peak known as the Mule in the west to the Carabas River. And you—all you were to inherit was the small manor house of Löwe and a mangy spinster named Kat. And you did inherit. First the house and me, and then the rest of it when your brothers died, and all without bothering to leave your precious war."

He wanted to sleep and the careless irritation that comes from being deprived of it was gnawing at his sense of preservation. "Did you truly expect me to leave my regiment and come home to a ramshackle old house to nursemaid the bastard daughter of some friend of my father's I don't even know? The French had entered the war? Old alliances were falling apart; new alliances were being formed. It was as if a puddle of mercury had dispersed into a hundred bubbles, some that would save you, others that would prove fatal." He shrugged, but had to look away from the winter in her eyes. "An ink-stained lawyer's clerk sent word that you were living with friends in the Tausend capital. It seemed adequate to me. I had more important things to deal with—such as a war."

"War or no, alliances or no—you still managed to turn inheriting this Kat into a profit, didn't you? A ten-thousand thaler profit! My marriage portion. But I didn't know that then, did I? No. I discovered it six years ago when word came that you were dead. At last! At age twenty-two I found myself mistress of my fortune and my fate—except, of course, that there was no fortune. That loss cost me dearly, von Löwe. But though you cost me while alive, by being dead you have managed to partially pay me back. Löwe Manor is mine."

memory niggled, but it was beyond grasping in his fuzzy head. Christ, she was beautiful. Full lips hinting at a sensual nature that belied the coldness in her eyes, the bones—if not her manner or her clothes—telling of well-bred nobility.

A former lover? Had he passed the long months of a year's winter quarters spending his passion in that glorious voluptuous body? One forgot a great many things in war, some by accident, others for the sake of sanity, but, sweet God, he'd take her gun and shoot himself if he could ever have forgotten that body—or those eyes.

Katharina von Melle. It felt as if he should remember it, but . . . nothing. "Madame von Melle, of course!" he prevaricated. "The wounds of war have addled my wits. Such eyes as those would be forever burned into any man's memor—" The slender finger curling on the trigger tightened. "I mean, that is—"

"I mean, that is . . . utter nonsense, Colonel von Löwe," she said, her gaze as steady as a cat's. "If there is any burning to be done, it will be into your body by a lead ball."

As a cat's . . . Katharina von Melle. Oh, Jesus.

"Kat," he said. "You're Father's Kat." They had never met, but he knew her. God save him, he knew her.

"You blanch quite nicely," she told him. "I take it you recognize the name? Your *ward,* my dear Colonel. I was your ward. First your father's, then *yours.* Do you remember now? I was part of your inheritance, remember? Your eldest brother was to get the north end of this valley, complete with the lucrative mill, your middle brother was to get all the land in the